FIERCE
&TRUE

DISCARD

FIERCE &TRUE

PLAYS FOR TEEN AUDIENCES

CHILDREN'S THEATRE COMPANY

PETER BROSIUS AND ELISSA ADAMS, EDITORS

UNIVERSITY OF MINNESOTA PRESS
MINNEAPOLIS
LONDON

The plays in this anthology were funded in part by The Wallace Foundation Leadership and Excellence in Arts Participation initiative, The Andrew W. Mellon Foundation, and The Harold and Mimi Steinberg Charitable Trust.

No performance or dramatic reading of any script or part thereof may be given without written permission. Inquiries may be addressed to Plays for Young Audiences, Children's Theatre Company, 2400 Third Avenue South, Minneapolis, MN 55404; by phone at 612-872-5108; or through e-mail at info@playsforyoungaudiences.org.

More information about Children's Theatre Company is available at www.childrenstheatre.org.

Published by the University of Minnesota Press
111 Third Avenue South, Suite 290
Minneapolis, MN 55401-2520
http://www.upress.umn.edu

Library of Congress Cataloging-in-Publication Data

Fierce and true : plays for teen audiences / Children's Theatre Company ;
Peter C. Brosius and Elissa Adams, editors.
    p. cm.
ISBN 978-0-8166-7310-0 (hc: alk. paper)
ISBN 978-0-8166-7311-7 (pbk: alk. paper)
1. Young adult drama, American.
2. Teenagers—Drama.
    I. Brosius, Peter.
    II. Adams, Elissa.
    III. Children's Theatre Company (Minneapolis, Minn.)
PS625.5.F54 2010
812'.60809283—dc22

2010025225

Printed in the United States of America on acid-free paper

The University of Minnesota is an equal-opportunity educator and employer.

17 16 15 14 13 12 11 10   10 9 8 7 6 5 4 3 2 1

CONTENTS

Peter Brosius

There is no great, long-standing canon of literature in the field of theatre for young people. Instead, it is a body of work being created in the here and now. A vital part of the mission of Children's Theatre Company (CTC) is to support the creation of new plays that are alive, theatrical, and speak to the immense imagination young people possess. New play development is a priority for CTC and involves an in-depth, long-range commitment to developing original work for young audiences. We commission leading artists from across this nation and around the world to write new plays springing from their history, vision, unique upbringing, or concerns they see in the lives of young people. When we adapt a classic story, we always ask ourselves how we can give the work the urgency and vitality it had when it was first imagined. After all, we are a theatre, not a museum.

Most of the writers in this anthology had never written specifically for teens before. We chose to work with them because we were excited by what could happen when these singular voices and this audience encountered and engaged one another. Our request was simple: write your best play ever. Don't write down to this audience, but be excited by the complexities, idiosyncrasies, and epic dilemmas in the lives of teenagers. There is a fantastic freedom of form for artists who write for young people, and many find that it reconnects them emotionally to the very reasons they became artists in the first place.

The writers whose work is collected here are as different as they could be from each other. Their styles, concerns, and aesthetics are so uniquely their own that the only thing binding them together is the excellence of their craft and the power of their storytelling. We hoped that a collision, a combustion, a new way of speaking to young people would emerge, and we have not been disappointed. We are thrilled to share this work with you. The plays will surprise you, take you to places you couldn't have imagined, and, we hope, redefine the field of theatre for young people.

These plays have all had a life on the stages of CTC. Many were developed over years, through conversation, workshops, readings, and rewrites. Staging these plays at CTC brought together leading directors, designers, and actors working in the theatre today. Established in 1965, Children's Theatre Company, located in Minneapolis, Minnesota, is widely recognized as the leading theatre for young people and families in North America. It has received numerous grants and awards recognizing its significant contribution to the field of theatre, including major support for its new plays for the Ford, Jerome, Joyce, Rockefeller, and Wallace foundations; the Children's Theatre Foundation of America Medallion; National Governor's Association; *Time* magazine's rating as the best children's theatre in the United States; and the 2003 Tony® Award for regional theatre. CTC exists to create extraordinary theatre experiences that educate, challenge, and inspire young people.

Our goal for *Fierce and True* is for these plays to be performed throughout the nation and the world and to excite audiences and artists about the unique possibilities of writing specifically for teenagers. These works have already touched many lives, lit fires in many imaginations, and encouraged audiences to think critically. This is a source of great joy for us at CTC: we hope that this anthology will become an invaluable resource for theatre professionals, educators, and especially teenagers who look to theatre as a place of challenge and inspiration.

INTRODUCTION: PLAYS FOR TEENS

Elissa Adams

For more than forty years, Children's Theatre Company earned its reputation as the flagship theatre for young people in the United States by staging plays that challenged and delighted children and their parents. But the children always grew up and out of what we offered onstage. Around the age of twelve, they either stopped attending theatre altogether or began attending the work geared for an adult audience at other theatres. We were losing an opportunity to engage with young people at a crucial and fascinating time in their lives. Thus, in 2003 we began to commission and produce work specifically for people ages twelve to eighteen.

We might have simply started a young adult series drawing on the extant theatrical canon—from Shakespeare and Chekhov to Neil Simon and Arthur Miller and Tony Kushner. But while this work is not *inappropriate* for teens to see, neither was it created with them in mind. CTC artistic director Peter Brosius recalls being in Europe in the 1980s when theatres like the Grips Theatre in Berlin and artists like Ad de Bont and Volker Ludwig were creating work designed to speak directly to teens. Brosius remembers the unique thrill of being in a theatre full of teenagers and watching them respond to the raucous, daring work the artists had created. It didn't feel like children's theatre, and it didn't feel like adult theatre. It felt like a whole new thing. Cultivating this age group as a distinct audience and creating work specifically for them is still a relatively new endeavor. Great work is being done by companies like Zeal Theatre in Australia, Canada's Green Thumb Theatre, Ontroerend Goed in the Netherlands, the Young Vic in the United Kingdom, and the Coterie Theatre here in the United States, but the body of theatrical literature for this age group is still in its own adolescence.

So the artistic team at CTC began to shape its vision for how to advance this body of work. One choice when creating plays for teens is to make plays *about* teens—to connect with them by mirroring their lives onstage. There is certainly a societal assumption that teenagers are particularly interested in themselves, that the teen years are a myopic, rather narcissistic time of life in which the focus is on identity, social status, and the insular world of school and friends. But we heard time and time again from teens that they didn't want to come and see their own immediate experience reflected back to them onstage. They live those things—they don't want to watch them in a theatre. They are more curious about the big, complex world of human relations and historical events than we sometimes assume.

Because artists are often the best interpreters of the great world of which teenagers are becoming aware, our exploration of what a play for teens can and should be has been led by the playwrights we commissioned. Whit MacLaughlin. Naomi Iizuka. Lonnie Carter. Will Power. We sought artists whose work had a ferocity, a contemporaneity, and a willingness to color outside the lines of well-made plays. We approached these artists and asked them to make plays for teens. The results are the four plays collected in this volume, which these artists created by marrying the call to write something that would appeal to twelve- to eighteen-year-olds to their own obsessions and aesthetics. All of these plays have teenage protagonists, but none can be easily categorized as a play *about* teens. They are successful because the artists tapped into a broader, richer understanding of this audience and made work for them that honors their sense of justice and their burgeoning interest in social activism, their understanding of history and global connections, their engagement with great works of literature, their awareness that, at this age, when they are no longer children, both the danger and the beauty of the world can and do affect them directly.

Teens have come to see these plays in greater numbers and with a stronger sense of enthusiasm and investment than we ever dared hope they would. They come with their teachers, with their friends, with their parents. They come in groups and on dates. They come back and see the plays again. They come not because these are plays *about* them, but because they are plays *for* them.

Prom was created in collaboration with New Paradise Laboratories (NPL), a Philadelphia-based experimental theatre company led by Whit MacLaughlin. Peter Brosius had seen NPL's *The Fab Four Reach the Pearly Gates* at a theatre conference and was wowed by it. NPL's work is highly physical and abstract, but it is infused with exploration of pop cultures and wild humor. The ensemble was attracting an audience of young people in their twenties, and Peter thought its work would speak to teens as well. In 2003, we invited MacLaughlin to CTC to work with teen performers and CTC's resident acting company. NPL uses a collective creative process, working with performers to shape the text, movement, and meaning of its plays. MacLaughlin and the actors began with the theme of embarrassment and the visual imagery of Pieter Brueghel the Elder's paintings. The result was *Prom*, what MacLaughlin calls "more of an experience than a play. It's a metaphysical look at a particularly American rite of passage ceremony." In *Prom*, the night plays out as an epic, athletic battle between students and chaperones. The prize is the keys to the future.

Playwright Naomi Iizuka has a history of reworking classic texts within contemporary contexts. Her play *Polaroid Stories* places street kids within the tales of Ovid's *Metamorphoses*; in *Skin*, Georg Büchner's character Woyzeck is a young soldier in a modern war. When we commissioned Iizuka to write a play for CTC, she gave us *Anon(ymous)*. Here, Homer's *Odyssey* is transposed onto an American landscape—a landscape as fraught with dangers and temptations as Homer's Aegean Sea, which Anon, a refugee from a war-torn country, must traverse as he seeks to be reunited with his mother. Iizuka says she wanted to create "a landscape that was both mythic and familiar, a landscape where Penelope is an immigrant working long hours in a sewing factory and Circe is a bartender in a seedy bar downtown."

The genesis of *The Lost Boys of Sudan* was an article in the *New York Times* magazine about the young men, most between the ages of eight and seventeen, left homeless when their parents were raped or killed and their lands burned during the civil war in the Sudan. Thousands of boys traveled across the Sudanese deserts to refugee camps and then on to resettlement in places as far-flung as Fargo, North Dakota. As chronicled in the article, these young men who had faced attacks by crocodiles and lions in the Sudan were now having to navigate a new life in a small, frigid midwestern town. Playwright Lonnie Carter came to our attention as the teller of this tale for the stage through our partnership with New Dramatists, a playwright organization based in New York. Carter's writing style is hallucinatory, free associative, and yet classical in its use of lineated verse and choral passages, and he has created an epitomic tale of youthful resilience for our century. But, as Carter says, "You come across a story like this and you realize that, even as an artist, your imagination pales in comparison to the truth. Everything that happens in this play is real."

Will Power's work combines the rhythm and politics of hip-hop with the narrative demands of theatre. When CTC commissioned him to write a play for teens, he wanted to make a piece rooted in the Minneapolis funk scene that would celebrate funk as the roots from which hip-hop grew and that harkened back to his own childhood. Peter Brosius had long wanted to do a piece about a teenage band. Out of that was born *The Five Fingers of Funk*, the story of a 1970s funk band whose high school players try to keep themselves and the band together even as politics, poverty, and parents threaten to break them apart. Together with composer Justin Ellington, Power took the idea of a play about a band one step further and crafted a play where the performers *are* the band. All of the songs in this musical are played live, in character, by the actors in their roles as band members of Five Fingers of Funk.

What are plays for teens? Plays for teens view twelve- to eighteen-year-olds as a viable and vibrant audience. They are written by playwrights of craft and passion. They may or may not be about teens, but they are plays that are fierce and true, ambitious, surprising, and complex. They are plays designed to engage and honor teen minds.

ANON(YMOUS)

Naomi Iizuka

An Adaptation of *The Odyssey*

The world premier of *Anon(ymous)* was directed by Peter Brosius and opened on April 4, 2006, at Children's Theatre Company. *Anon(ymous)* was funded in part by The Joyce Foundation and the National Endowment for the Arts.

CREATIVE TEAM
Scenic design: Kate Edmunds
Costume design: Christal Weatherly
Lighting design: Geoff Korf
Music and sound design: Andre Pluess and Ben Sussmann
Dramaturgy: Elissa Adams
Video design: Rebecca Fuller
Fight choreographer: Edward "Ted" Sharon
Stage manager: Jenny R. Friend

CAST

NEMASANI	Rosanna Ma
ANON	Michael Escamilla
MR. YURI MACKUS, STRYGAL, LONE BARFLY	Terry Hempleman
SENATOR LAIUS, MR. ZYCLO, NICE AMERICAN FATHER	Steve Hendrickson
HELEN LAIUS, MR. ZYCLO'S PET BIRD, NICE AMERICAN MOTHER	Annie Enneking
CALISTA, SEWING LADY 3, NICE AMERICAN DAUGHTER	Becka Ollmann
NAJA	Sonja Parks
PROTEUS, ALI, IGNACIO	Emil Herrara
NASREEN, SEWING LADY 2, BELEN	Hadija Steen-Omari
RITU, SEWING LADY 1, SERZA	Marvette Knight
PASCAL	Gavin Lawrence

1

++

Light on ANON.

ANON: Where I come from is far away from here.

CHORUS OF REFUGEES *emerge from the darkness.*

CHORUS: Where I come from is oxen in rice fields and hills the
                    color of green tea.
               Where I come from is jungles filled with jaguars and
                    pythons thick as a grown man's thigh.
               Where I come from is poison frogs the size of a
                    thumbnail and squirrels that can fly from tree
                    to tree.
               Where I come from is waterfalls taller than the tallest
                    skyscraper
               is olive trees and ancient desert
               is sampans and temple bell
               is sandstorms
               is monsoon rains
               is tapir and okapi and electric blue butterflies with
                    wings as wide as my arms.
               where I come from is the smell of orchid and mango and
                    ripe papaya
               is the smell of my mother's fried bread
               is the smell of yerba maté

lemongrass
horchata
coconut milk
pho
fried squid
cow's blood
joss stick
sheep's milk, fresh and warm.
The sounds of war begin, faint and distant.

CHORUS: Where I come from is high up in the mountains where
the sound of thunder is so loud it sounds like the
end of the world.
Where I come from is the edge of an ocean so blue you
can see straight to the bottom, and the sound of the
waves crashing sounds like the end of the world.
Where I come from giant birds circle overhead, so many
you can't count them all, they come and they come
till the sky is black with birds, they caw caw caw, and
the sound they make is so loud, it sounds like the
end of the world.

The CHORUS OF REFUGEES *disperses in all different directions.* NAJA
remains. The sounds of war grow closer.

NAJA: Do you remember?
ANON: No—
NAJA: All those memories—
ANON: I don't remember—
NAJA: Can you hear them—
ANON: No—
NAJA: You can't hear them, all those memories inside of you?
You've locked them inside for so long, and now they're pounding
against your rib cage, against the walls of your heart. Can you
hear them? Listen.

Whispered fragments from the first chorus. The sounds of war grow closer.

ANON: I don't know how to begin. I don't know where to begin.

NAJA: Sssssssh.
        Begin in the middle,
        on the border,
        on the crossing.
        Begin in the place in between.

NAJA *begins to recede from view. Night falls. The sky is vast and inky blue.
The sounds of war grow closer. Gunfire. The whistling of bombs falling
from the sky.*
    ANON *is alone in the night.*

ANON: Where I come from is far away from here.
            Where I come from there was a war that lasted so long
                people forgot what they were fighting for.
            Where I come from bombs rained down from the sky
                night after night
            and boys wandered the streets with M16s.
            Where I come from mines are planted in the roads like
                deadly flowers,
            and the air smells like death, rank and sticky sweet.
            Where I come from you go to sleep at night and dream
                about the faces of the people you love.

Light on NEMASANI. *She sings an ancient song.* ANON *sees her; she
doesn't see him.*

ANON: You dream the face of the one person you love. And that
        person, that person becomes like home. Their eyes. Their skin.
        Their voice, the sound of their voice. And so you dream about
        that person. You dream about home. You dream about going
        home.

ANON *approaches* NEMASANI. *The sounds of war get so loud. It sounds like the end of the world. The whistling sound of a bomb falling from the sky. The whistling grows louder, closer.* NAJA *emerges from the darkness. She pulls* ANON *out of the path of the bomb. They leap into a vast, uncharted darkness. An explosion. Blinding white light. The sounds of war transform into the sound of sewing machines.*

A sewing factory in a city somewhere in America. The sound of the sewing machines like a hive of metallic bumblebees. A mountain of fabric reaching up to the heavens. Rows of sewing machines one after the next as far as the eye can see. The CHORUS OF SEWING LADIES *sews in perfect unison.* NEMASANI *is one of the* SEWING LADIES. *She sews a shroud.* MR. YURI MACKUS *is the manager of the sewing factory. He escorts* SENATOR *and* MRS. (HELEN) LAIUS *around the factory floor.*

MR. YURI MACKUS (*to* SENATOR LAIUS): The first thing I want to
   say is that we are not a sweatshop. We are the first stop on the
   way to the American dream. Give us your poor, your huddled
   masses yearning to be free—and we'll hire them. We'll give them
   a job. We'll put them to work. Nothing wrong with good honest
   work. As you can see, Senator, the conditions here are first rate.
   Light and airy. Modern. Cheerful. We have a great time. Don't
   we, ladies? All the ladies love me and I love them.
SENATOR LAIUS (*to the* SEWING LADIES): Don't mind us please
   don't mind us. We're just here to observe.
HELEN LAIUS (*to the* SEWING LADIES): What are you making?

SEWING LADIES: blue jeans
                 T-shirts
                 yoga pants
                 sports bras
                 boxer shorts
                 warm-up jackets
                 polo shirts
                 tube socks
                 short shorts
                 sweatshirts

khaki pants

baseball caps

miniskirts

baby bonnets

oxford shirts

bikini tops

HELEN LAIUS (*seeing* NEMASANI's *shroud*): Ooooh I love this.
What is it?

NEMASANI: A shroud.

HELEN LAIUS: Ooooh a shroud. How interesting. What's a shroud?

NEMASANI: It's a sheet you wrap around the dead.

HELEN LAIUS: Oh. Oh I see. And do you sell a lot of those? Shrouds,
I mean.

NEMASANI: It's not for sale.

HELEN LAIUS: It's lovely, the design is just lovely. I collect primitive
art, you know, from all around the world. It's a passion of
mine. I have baskets from Guatemala and little Buddhas from
Cambodia. They speak to me. This speaks to me. I would love to
buy this and hang it on my wall.

NEMASANI: It's not for sale.

MR. MACKUS: Don't mind Penny.

NEMASANI: My name's not Penny.

MR. MACKUS: Her real name is too hard to pronounce. We call her
Penny. It's easier. Isn't it, Penny?

SEWING LADY 1: Mr. Mackus wants to marry Penny. He proposes to
her every day. "Will you marry me, Penny," he whispers in her
ear. He gets so close she can smell his breath. Coffee and tic tacs.
She tells him she'll say yes when she finishes the shroud.

MR. MACKUS: I love Penny. I want to give her a good home. She's
had a very hard life. I'm just doing my part. I have a big heart.
It's my undoing.

SEWING LADY 1: Mr. Mackus had a mail-order bride from Russia . . .

MR. MACKUS: Not true—

SEWING LADY 1: . . . and one from the Philippines . . .

MR. MACKUS: Lies lies all lies—

SEWING LADY 1: . . . and one from Thailand, Romania, and Honduras . . .

MR. MACKUS: THAT'S ENOUGH!

HELEN LAIUS: Who's it for? The shroud, I mean.

NEMASANI: My son.

HELEN LAIUS: Your son? Is he dead? That's so sad. That makes me very, very sad.

SENATOR LAIUS: Helen, darling—

HELEN LAIUS: You must be devastated. You poor thing. How did he die? You can tell me.

NEMASANI: He drowned.

HELEN LAIUS: He drowned! That's awful. It's so tragic, it's just so tragic. I feel your pain, I really do. How did it happen? If you don't mind me asking. It helps sometimes to talk, you know, to share. That's what human beings do, they share, they share their joy, they share their pain, it's only human, we're only human, you can tell me, go on tell me—and maybe I can help.

The sewing factory transforms into the ocean.

Nemasani (Rosanna Ma) recounts the story of her journey to America in Naomi Iizuka's contemporary telling of *The Odyssey* in the world premiere of *Anon(ymous)* (2006). Photograph by Rob Levine.

Night. The ocean. Light on ANON. *He holds a toy boat, which he steers through a dark ocean. It's night.*

NEMASANI: Where we come from, there was a war. And my son and me, we escaped. We escaped in the middle of the night. We sailed out to sea in an old fishing boat. There were so many people all crammed together, old people and little babies. We huddled together in the dark in the belly of the ship. We listened to the roar of the waves. We listened to the boat creak and moan. And then the storm started.

The storm begins. Lightning. Thunder claps.

NEMASANI: The winds began to howl. The sky opened up and the rain came down, sheets and sheets of rain. And the lightning lit up the sky, bright bright light, and the thunder crashed. And the sound was so loud. And suddenly a giant wave rose up. It rose and it rose like a wall of water, and then it fell over us and swallowed us whole.

The wave crashes down. Darkness.

The sound of the surf. Light up on a tropical beach somewhere in America. A boy named ANON. *A girl named* CALISTA. CALISTA *wears a bathing suit.* ANON *wears street clothes.* ANON *examines the broken toy boat.* CALISTA *has a camera. She takes pictures. Music plays on a portable CD player.*

ANON: Someday I'm going to sail away.
CALISTA: No you're not. Don't be silly. You're not going anywhere. This is your home now.
ANON: It's not my home.
CALISTA: Yes, it is.
ANON: It's not my real home.
CALISTA: Yes, it is. Now look at me. Look at me. Smile. I SAID SMILE.

CALISTA *snaps a photo of* ANON.

CALISTA: You're very photogenic. You could be a male model. You're so swarthy and exotic. That's very in right now. Exotic is very in. I wish I were more exotic. I'm too pale. I wish I had a tan. I wish my skin was the color of café au lait.

A new song begins on the portable CD player.

CALISTA: Ooooh I love this song. Do you want to watch TV? We could watch TV on my giant flat-screen plasma TV. It's so cool. It's so flat.
ANON: No thanks.
CALISTA: What about a snack?

CALISTA *retrieves a bag of candies. She begins to eat. She eats a lot. She stuffs her face with candy.*

CALISTA: I have M&M's and Kit Kats and Nestlé's Crunch and Snickers and Reese's Pieces and Charleston Chews and Sweet Tarts and Lemonheads and Skittles and Spree.
ANON: I'm not hungry.
CALISTA: Suit yourself. We could do something else. We could kiss. You could kiss me. Do you want to kiss me?
ANON: No.
CALISTA: That's OK. You can kiss me later.
ANON: I'm never going to kiss you.
CALISTA: Fine.
ANON: Not now or later. Not ever.
CALISTA: FINE! *(Pause.)* Why are you so mean to me? You should be nice to me. I saved your life. You washed up on the shore of my dad's luxury beachfront condo and you weren't even breathing. I fished seaweed out of your mouth. I administered CPR; I gave you the kiss of life just like I learned in summer camp. And I thought you were so handsome and exotic and not like any of the boys from around here. I saved your life, and you're so ungrateful! You won't even tell me your real name!

ANON: I told you my real name.

CALISTA: Your real name is not "nobody." What kind of mom names their kid "nobody"?

ANON: Don't talk about my mom.

CALISTA: I mean I'm sure she was nice and all, but it's not even like she's even part of your life anymore. I mean she's probably dead, and even if she's alive, it's not like she's been trying that hard to find you. Honestly, if you want my opinion, she's probably moved on with her life. I know I would. I bet if you showed up on her doorstep like right this second, she probably wouldn't even know who you were. She'd probably be like: "Who are you? Do I know you?"

ANON: I SAID DON'T TALK ABOUT MY MOM! (*Pause.*) OK look, I can't stay here anymore. I can't do it.

CALISTA: Why not? It's nice here. It's pretty and clean. And I have satellite TV.

ANON: I gotta go. I'm going to lose my mind if I have to stay here one more day.

CALISTA: Where would you go?

ANON: Home.

CALISTA: But this is your home.

ANON: My real home.

CALISTA: Your "real home"? That's crazy. Your "real home" is a dirty little third-world shack with no running water. It's raw sewage in the streets and malaria and cholera and all kinds of disgusting parasites I don't even want to think about. I'm just saying how it is. Don't be mad. Now you're mad. Let's kiss and make up.

ANON: No.

CALISTA: Why not?

ANON: Because I hate you, and every time you open your mouth I want to stuff sand down your throat.

CALISTA: OK, you know what? I don't care. I don't care what you think. I don't care what you want. You will eat my Skittles and my Kit Kats and my Spree. You will enjoy my flat-screen plasma TV. And you will love me.

Enter NAJA *from the ocean. She's a surfer. She wears a wet suit. She has a surfboard.*

NAJA: Hey.

ANON: Hey.

NAJA: Remember me?

ANON: Yeah. Kinda.

CALISTA: Where did you come from?

NAJA: He called me.

ANON: I did?

NAJA: He sent telepathic brain waves out into the universe and I was listening.

ANON: You were?

NAJA: I was. I'm a really, really good listener.

ANON: That's cool.

NAJA: I know.

ANON: That's really cool.

NAJA: I know.

CALISTA: Uh, excuse me. Who are you?

NAJA: I'm a goddess. And you are?

CALISTA: I live here. My dad owns this place. He owns everything as far as the eye can see. He's very, very powerful. That's who I am.

NAJA: Is that supposed to impress me?

CALISTA: I'm just saying how it is.

NAJA: You know? You're like really pale.

CALISTA: Yeah? Well you're like really rude.

NAJA: Yeah, but you're really pale. How does a person get to be so pale? You're like Wonder Bread. You're like mayonnaise.

CALISTA: I am not like mayonnaise. Cow.

NAJA: Hag.

CALISTA: Witch.

NAJA *pulls* CALISTA's *hair.*

CALISTA: OW! This is a private beach. So you better just take your stupid surfboard and take a hike.

NAJA: You can't own a beach.

CALISTA: Yes, you can. My dad does. My dad owns the beach and the whole entire ocean.

NAJA: That's the stupidest thing I've ever heard. That's like saying you own a jungle or a mountain range.

CALISTA: My dad owns some of those, too. My dad is very rich.

NAJA: Yeah? Well, if he's so rich, maybe he can buy you a better bathing suit. 'Cause that bathing suit is ugly.

CALISTA: Shut up.

NAJA: It's like the ugliest bathing suit I've ever seen.

CALISTA: Shut up!

NAJA *(to* ANON*)*: So you want to go or what?

ANON: Like now?

NAJA: Like right now, like right this second.

CALISTA: He's not going anywhere. He's not allowed.

NAJA: He's "not allowed"? Who says?

CALISTA: My dad. My dad says we have to stay inside our luxury-gated community. My dad says it's dangerous out there. My dad says all these foreigners are flooding in with all their strange customs and their weird food, and they don't speak English, and they're not like us, and most of them are illegal, they're illegal aliens, that's what my dad says. Whenever he says that, I think of little green men in space suits, but that's not the kind of alien he means, it's a different kind of alien.

NAJA: You're an idiot.

CALISTA: Shut up.

NAJA: And your dad's an even bigger idiot.

CALISTA: My dad is not an idiot. My dad is really, really rich and really, really powerful. And you don't want to make him mad.

NAJA: Look, I don't care about your dad. I don't care what he thinks or says or does. I don't listen to people like your dad. And he doesn't either. *(To* ANON.*)* Right?

ANON: Right.

NAJA: Ready?

ANON: Yeah.

CALISTA: Wait. You can't go.

ANON: Yeah, I can. Watch me.

ANON *and* NAJA *dive into the ocean.*

CALISTA: Wait! Stop! Come back! I'm going to call my dad! And then you're going to be sorry!

CALISTA*'s voice becomes a tiny echo fainter and fainter.* CALISTA *becomes a tiny figure on the shore, a speck too small to see.*

The middle of a giant ocean. ANON *and* NAJA *are floating. It's very calm.*

ANON: The last time I was in the ocean, I almost drowned.

NAJA: I know.

ANON: I was with my mom. We were in an old fishing boat. We were trying to escape and there was a storm—

NAJA: I know.

ANON: How could you know that?

NAJA: You don't remember me, do you?

ANON: Yeah, I do. We knew each other when we were kids.

NAJA: Oh yeah?

ANON: Yeah. You lived across the street.

NAJA: Is that right?

ANON: Yeah. You lived in a big old building. It's not there anymore. The bombs fell and it was destroyed.

NAJA: I know. *(Pause.)* What was I like?

ANON: Kinda shy. Kinda cute. Your hair was different.

NAJA: Shorter? Longer?

ANON: Just different. I had a crush on you.

NAJA: Oh yeah?

ANON: Yeah.

NAJA: I think you're thinking of someone else.

ANON: Maybe. *(Pause.)* OK. I think I remember now. You were this girl at the airport.

NAJA: Yeah?

ANON: You were waiting to get on a plane. You were going somewhere faraway. You were all by yourself. You were reading a book.

NAJA: What book?

ANON: It was a big book. I remember it was like this really big, old book. It was really, really big. The title is on the tip of my tongue.

NAJA: You don't remember me.

ANON: No. Not really. But I feel like I do. I feel like I know you. I feel like I've known you my whole life.

NAJA: That's because I'm a goddess and I come to you in your dreams.

ANON: Really?

NAJA: Uh huh. And you're a mere mortal so you don't remember. Your brain's too small.

ANON: Is that how it works?

NAJA: Pretty much.

ANON: And what do you do? Like when you come to me in my dreams?

NAJA: I give you advice. I whisper it in your ear. Sometimes I save your life.

ANON: Is that right?

NAJA: Uh huh.

ANON *and* NAJA *kiss.*

ANON: Do all goddesses kiss like that?

NAJA: No, just me.

ANON *and* NAJA *kiss.*

ANON: I'm really homesick.

NAJA: I know.

ANON: It's like a big empty room inside of me.

NAJA: I know.

ANON: What if you want to go home, but there's no more home to go home to? What if the one person you love more than anything, what if they don't remember you? What if they don't even know who you are?

NAJA: Sssssssh.

NAJA *kisses* ANON. NAJA *pulls away.*

NAJA: OK, no more kissing. You have things to do.

ANON: Like what?

NAJA: Like survive the storm.

ANON: Why does there always have to be a storm? Why can't it just be smooth sailing?

NAJA: Don't ask why. Just start swimming.

The winds pick up. The clouds race. The sky darkens. The waves rise. A blinding light. A lightning flash. A clap of thunder.

ANON: Wait!

ANON *and* NAJA *are hurled in different directions.*

The ocean transforms into the sewing factory. The end of the day. The sewing factory is deserted. HELEN LAIUS *and* NEMASANI *are alone.* HELEN *has been listening to* NEMASANI's *story.*

HELEN LAIUS: And your little boy? Did you ever see him again?

NEMASANI: No. Sometimes I think maybe he was saved. Maybe the coast guard found him. Or maybe he was able to swim to shore.

HELEN LAIUS: Wouldn't that be something.

NEMASANI: And then maybe he was adopted by a nice American family.

HELEN LAIUS: Yes! We adopted a little boy from the third world. The senator and I found him in a refugee camp. He was so cute. We had such high hopes. But it didn't work out. He was nothing but problems from the start. He didn't blend in. He had a bad attitude. And then he ran away. Can you believe it? We gave him everything and he ran away.

NEMASANI: I think maybe my son, maybe he's alive somewhere.

HELEN LAIUS: Maybe. Probably not. But maybe.

SENATOR LAIUS *and* MR. MACKUS *appear.*

SENATOR LAIUS: Helen, darling, we really have to scoot.

HELEN LAIUS: I hope it all works out for you. I really do.

SENATOR LAIUS: Helen—

HELEN LAIUS: I mean I hope you can find closure and renewal. I find
meditation and yoga, yoga can be really helpful, mindfulness
and deep breathing—

SENATOR LAIUS: Helen!

HELEN LAIUS: Coming, darling.

HELEN LAIUS *and* SENATOR LAIUS *exit.* NEMASANI *returns to sewing the
shroud.* MR. MACKUS *is holding bags of takeout.*

MR. MACKUS: Mmmm. I ordered some takeout for the two of us.
It's from this Indian place on the other side of town. I got us
a little chicken tikka masala, a little papadum, a little naan.
mmmm. Taste.

NEMASANI: I'm not hungry.

MR. MACKUS: Marry me, you little vixen, you little minx.

NEMASANI: Mr. Mackus.

MR. MACKUS: You know you want to marry me. You find me
irresistible.

NEMASANI: Mr. Mackus, please.

MR. MACKUS: This "playing hard to get," Penny, is getting really old.
You either marry me or lose your job. I hate to be so blunt, but
that's the way it is.

NEMASANI: Mr. Mackus, as I told you, in my homeland, it is
customary—

MR. MACKUS: Yes yes yes, "it is customary to make a shroud in which
to bury the dead."

NEMASANI: That's correct.

MR. MACKUS: Yes, but who's dead? You're not dead. I'm not dead. We're alive, Penny. We're vital. We have needs and desires. We have appetites—

NEMASANI: Mr. Mackus—

NEMASANI *smacks the advancing* MR. MACKUS.

MR. MACKUS: OW!

NEMASANI: When I am done, we can get married.

MR. MACKUS: Can't you speed things up?

NEMASANI: It takes as long as it takes.

MR. MACKUS: What if I can't wait?

NEMASANI: Then you will incur the wrath of the gods. Bad luck like you has never seen before. Forget about the number thirteen. Forget about breaking a mirror or stepping on a crack. Do you want to tempt fate, Mr. Mackus? Do you know what happens to mortals who tempt fate? Vultures pecking at your liver and your eyeballs for all eternity. Your arms and legs ripped from their sockets, your head pried loose from its neck. Your skull smashed against a rock, brain goo splattered all over the pavement—

MR. MACKUS: Fine. No need to agitate the gods. My little crab apple. My little peach pit. I'll wait. I can wait. Sweet dreams, my little sweet potato.

Exit MR. MACKUS. *When* NEMASANI *is sure he is gone, she begins to undo the stitches of the shroud.* SEWING LADY 2 *peeks out from behind a sewing machine and sees what* NEMASANI *is doing.*

A police helicopter overhead. The chup chup chup sound of its propellers. A bright beam of light shines down. Night in a city somewhere in America. The sounds of a city at night. Freeway traffic. A constant twinkling stream of tiny cars. TVs and voices and the clanking of garbage cans and the beep beep beep of trucks backing up. Somewhere in the giant city, the sound of a song from somewhere faraway. NAJA *enters with a transistor radio from which the song is playing. She sets the radio down.*

The song continues. An alley behind an Indian restaurant. A neon sign spelling "CURRY." NASREEN *opens the back door with a bag of garbage. She tosses the garbage bag into the dumpster. She sees the radio. She approaches the radio. She sings along briefly to the song.* NASREEN *hears a sound coming from the dumpster.* ANON *appears from out of the trash in the dumpster.* NASREEN *grabs the radio to use as a weapon.*

ANON: I didn't mean to scare you.

NASREEN: You didn't scare me.

ANON: You look kinda scared.

NASREEN: Well I'm not.

ANON: Are you sure?

NASREEN: Yes.

ANON: You shouldn't be hanging out in dark alleys in the middle of the night. It's dangerous.

NASREEN: I don't care. I'm strong.

ANON: You don't look that strong.

NASREEN: Well I am.

ANON: It's OK. I mean you'd be OK no matter what, cause I'd protect you.

NASREEN: I don't need protecting.

ANON: Right, cause you're strong.

NASREEN: That's right. I am.

ANON: I believe you.

NASREEN: Good.

Pause. The song on the radio plays.

ANON: You have a nice voice.

NASREEN: No I don't.

RITU (*off*): NASREEN!

ANON: I like that song you were singing.

NASREEN: It's old. It's the kinda stuff my mom listens to. My mom has a nice voice. She sings. I don't sing.

RITU (*off*): NASREEN!

NASREEN: What's your name?

ANON (*seeing the "CURRY" sign*): Koo Ri.

NASREEN: I never heard that name before. What does it mean?

ANON: Quick-thinking.

NASREEN: Is it stinky in there?

ANON: Kinda. But the food's pretty good.

NASREEN: What food?

ANON *lifts up a to-go carton from the dumpster.*

NASREEN: That's not food. That's garbage.

ANON: What makes it garbage?

NASREEN: It's in the garbage can.

ANON: Yeah, but it's the same food. It's just in a different setting.

NASREEN: Sometimes, the customers order all this food and then
   they take just one bite, and they say it's too spicy, and so they
   send it back, and then we have to throw it away.

ANON: I like spicy.

NASREEN: Me, too. The hotter the better.

RITU (*off*): NASREEN!

ALI (*off*): Nasreen, what are you up to? Your mother has been calling
   and calling.

Enter ALI. *He is blind. He makes his way over to* ANON.

ALI: Are you conversing with the cockroaches? What do the
   cockroaches have to say for themselves this evening? Perhaps
   they say: "Hello, Nasreen. How are you? Did you bring me some
   leftover curry or a few morsels of naan?"

ALI *is very close to* ANON. *He stops. He sniffs.*

ALI: You're very pungent, Mr. Cockroach. I smell a whiff of our
   delicious aloo gobi from last week. And there, there is our
   delectable chicken korma from just yesterday. And right there
   is our mouth-watering lamb saag. I have an excellent sense of
   smell. Do you speak?

ANON: Yeah.

ALI: Remarkable. A very large cockroach endowed with the gift of speech.

ANON: I'm not a cockroach.

ALI: Good. That's good. My wife kills cockroaches, you know. She crushes them with her shoe.

NASREEN: His name is Koo Ri.

ALI: Koo Ri?

NASREEN: Yes.

ANON: Look I should probably go—

ALI: I'm Ali.

ANON: Nice to meet you, Mr. Ali, but—

ALI: Not Mr. Ali, just Ali. And this is my lovely daughter Nasreen. You've already met. I am the proprietor of this establishment. My wife, Ritu, is the chef. Each dish she makes is a masterpiece. The scents, the tastes of home in each delicious bite.

ANON: Look I really gotta go—

ALI: You will be our guest.

ANON: That's really nice of you, but I can't. I really have to get going—

ALI: I insist. I assure you it's more comfortable indoors. This way, please—

ANON: No see I can't do that. I can't stay—

ALI: Nonsense. Nasreen, set a table for our guest. Ritu, we have company!

ALI ushers ANON inside. NASREEN follows.

The kitchen of an Indian restaurant. Steam and the sound of running water. Dishes piled high. The sound of chopping and the clattering of silverware and china. The hiss of the fry pan. A gust of flame. RITU is cooking. ALI and NASREEN sit at a table full of assorted hot peppers. ANON watches them from the edge of the room. ALI pops a pepper in his mouth.

ALI: It's so hot. It's hot hot hot. It's so hot I want to cry.

RITU: Ali, you're going to give yourself a bellyache.

ALI: Nonsense. I can take it.

ALI *pops another pepper in his mouth.*

RITU: Ali, stop. You're going to keel over.

ALI *(gasping)*: It's the pepper. It makes me sweat. It's very healthy.

RITU: You're turning red like a beet. Tell me this is healthy.

ALI: Very healthy.

NASREEN: It's so little.

ALI: Don't be fooled. It's the hottest pepper of them all.

RITU: Enough is enough. You eat that pepper, your tongue will fall out of your mulish old head.

NASREEN: What about our guest, poppa? Maybe he wants to try.

ANON: No, that's OK.

NASREEN: I thought you said you like spicy.

ANON: I do.

NASREEN *(holding out the pepper)*: Well, here you go.

ALI: Nasreen—

NASREEN: But he said he liked spicy. That's what he said. Isn't that what you said?

ALI: Nasreen, my dove, there's spicy, and then there's spicy. I think our guest is wise enough to know the difference.

NASREEN: I think he's scared.

ANON: I'm not scared. How bad can it be?

NASREEN: Bad.

ALI: A burning inferno.

NASREEN: The death star of peppers.

ANON *pops the pepper in his mouth.*

ALI: Well?

ANON *opens his mouth. Proof he swallowed.*

NASREEN: He did it.

ALI: Impressive, stranger. I'm impressed.

RITU: I used to have a goat that could eat anything. Tin cans. Hubcaps. Hot peppers.

NASREEN: You did? What happened to him?

RITU: I chopped him up and made goat stew.

ALI: Ritu.

RITU: Where do you come from, stranger?

ANON: I'm from all over.

RITU: And your family? Where are they?

ANON: I don't know. I'm not sure.

RITU: I see. And what was your name again? I don't think I caught it.

ANON: Nobody. I mean Koo Ri. I mean, nobody. I mean, I mean Koo Ri.

RITU: Koo Ri or nobody, which is it?

ANON: Nobody. I'm nobody.

RITU: Cooking for nobody, am I? That seems like a waste of perfectly good food.

ALI: Ritu, please.

RITU: You're too trusting, Ali. The city is full of liars and thieves. We don't know him. We don't know where he comes from. We don't know anything about him.

ANON: She's right. I should go. I'm really sorry—

ALI: No. You are our guest. Ritu has had a long day. Please forgive her.

RITU: Ritu has had many long days. Ritu has had many long weeks and months and years. And Ritu can speak for herself. *(To* ANON.*)* Here. I cooked it, you might as well eat it.

RITU *sets a plate of food down in front of* ANON. *She sets it down hard.*

ANON: Thanks. Thank you.

ANON *eats in silence.* RITU *and* NASREEN *clean up.*

ANON: Cumin, cinnamon, nutmeg, turmeric. Allspice, cardamom, fennel, clove . . . coriander.

RITU: Yes, coriander. How did you know that?

ANON: My mom used the same spices. She just put them together differently.

NASREEN: Where is she now?

ANON: I don't know.

NASREEN: How can you not know where your mom is?

ANON: Where I come from, there was a war. There was a war, and lots of people disappeared.

NASREEN: You mean they died.

RITU: Nasreen—

ANON: Some of them. But some of them, they just, they disappeared.

NASREEN: Maybe they escaped.

ANON: Maybe.

NASREEN: Maybe your mom escaped. Maybe she's living in the city somewhere, and you just don't know it because she changed her name, but she's looking for you, too, only she doesn't know where to look because she came here from somewhere else, so she doesn't know how to get around. Lots of people come here from someplace else. We did. Where we came from, there was a war, too.

RITU: Nasreen—

NASREEN: That's how my dad became blind. There was a bomb in the marketplace. Lots of people died, old people and little children—

RITU: Nasreen, that's enough. That was before. We don't talk about that now.

NASREEN: I don't remember where we came from. I was just a baby when we left.

ALI: You remember. You just don't remember that you remember.

NASREEN: How can I remember what I don't remember?

NAJA *enters. She's unseen and unheard by everyone except for* ANON.

ALI: Sometimes in your dreams, something will bubble up from the depths, a tiny flicker of something you thought you forgot. A taste or a scent—

RITU: Jasmine.

ALI: Yes, jasmine.

NAJA *turns on the radio. An ancient song from faraway.* ALI *caresses* RITU*'s hair.*

ALI: Your mother used to wear jasmine blossoms in her hair. I come across that scent sometimes, and it takes me back. All of a sudden I think of something from years before, some tiny thing. A piece of a memory, like a shiny coin at the bottom of a well.

NASREEN *approaches* RITU *and* ALI. RITU *wraps her arms around her daughter.* ANON *watches the family from a distance.* NAJA *approaches* ANON.

NAJA: What do you remember?

The sounds of distant war.

ANON: I don't know where to begin. I don't know how. I don't know how to begin.

NAJA: Begin in the middle,
          on the border,
          on the crossing.
          Begin in the place in between.

The sounds of distant war grow closer. NAJA, ALI, RITU, *and* NASREEN *recede from view.*

ANON *remembers. Chaos in a burning city far away. The sound of rockets and mortars. Lightning. Thunder. The city transforms into an ocean. A tiny boat on a giant ocean. Night. He sees* NEMASANI. *She sings the same wordless melody she sang before.*

ANON: I remember my mom. And how she used to hold me.
          She held me when the bombs fell.
          She held me when the ground shook and the city
              burned.

She held me on the night that we escaped.

She held me in the belly of the boat as we sailed across a
giant sea.

I remember how she held me.

And then one night there was a terrible storm.

A storm at sea. Winds howling. Sheets of rain. A terrible cracking sound.
The boat splits apart. An explosion of water. NEMASANI *vanishes under a*
giant wave.

The roar of the surf. ANON *is in the ocean. Water as far as the eye can*
see. Night. Tiny lights shimmer in the distance.

ANON: The next thing I remember: I was floating in a giant ocean.
In the distance, I could see tiny lights. I started swimming
toward them. I swam even though my clothes were soaked
through and my arms and legs were numb, even though it hurt
to breathe. I swam and I swam. I swam until I couldn't swim
anymore. And then everything went black.

Blackout. Everything is darkness.

PASCAL: Psst. Wake up. Wake up. Quick. Come on.

The sound of a siren. Shouts. The sound of footsteps on pavement, on steel
containers. The clank of chain-link. The sound of running. ANON *and*
PASCAL *are running through the darkness. Glare of headlights. The sound*
of a city. They run. They run. They run.

A tunnel underground. Graffiti and a giant L & N painted on the
wall. The sound of rats. PASCAL *and* ANON *catch their breath.* PASCAL *is*
West African. He has traditional scars on his face, thin horizontal lines.

PASCAL: They won't come after us here.
ANON: Who were they?
PASCAL: Police. I.N.S. Rent-a-cop. Who knows?
ANON: Where are we?

PASCAL: Tunnel.

ANON: What's that sound?

PASCAL: Rats. Giant rats. Five foot long, nose to tail. They live down here. They eat human flesh. They got a taste for it. They hunt for humans in the night. They go in packs. And if they find you alone and sleeping, they attack. They rip you to shreds. They tear out your insides. They rip out your still beating heart.

ANON: I didn't know rats came that big.

PASCAL: What? You don't believe me.

ANON: No.

PASCAL: Liar. You're scared. I can see it in your eyes.

ANON: I'm not scared.

PASCAL: Yeah you are. You ran like a little girl just now.

ANON: Then that makes two of us.

PASCAL: Come again?

ANON: I said that makes two of us. Little girl.

PASCAL: I'm not a little girl.

ANON: No you're right. You're just a blowhard.

PASCAL: What did you say to me?

ANON: You heard me. Blowhard.

PASCAL *rushes* ANON. *They fight. They fight. And then eventually they stop. A draw. They sit in the dirt in silence.*

ANON: Why did you help me? Before, I mean.

PASCAL: I don't know. I guess you looked like you needed some help.

ANON: Thanks.

PASCAL: Whatever.

They sit in silence. PASCAL *pulls out potato chips from his bag.*

PASCAL: Hungry?

ANON: Yeah.

PASCAL *shares his bag of potato chips with* ANON. *They eat.*

PASCAL: Where did you learn English?

ANON: My mom, she taught me.

PASCAL: Yeah?

ANON: Yeah.

PASCAL: I'm Pascal.

ANON (*seeing the L & N sign*): I'm Lan.

PASCAL: Lan, huh?

ANON: Yeah. Lan.

PASCAL *and* ANON *stare each other down.* ANON*'s eyes drift to the scars on* PASCAL*'s face.*

PASCAL: Didn't nobody tell you it's rude to stare.

ANON: Sorry.

PASCAL: Where I come from, they cut your face when you turn thirteen. Like a warrior. You got any scars?

ANON: No.

PASCAL: Everybody got scars. Maybe yours you just can't see.

A shadow emerges from the darkness looking for food. ANON *starts for him.*

PASCAL (*holding* ANON *back*): Don't. He don't hurt no one. He lives down there.

ANON: What's wrong with him?

PASCAL: What's wrong with him? He's high. He's high as a kite.

ANON: He looks like someone I know.

PASCAL: Yeah? He could be. He won't remember if he is. His brain is fried. He don't remember nothing. He don't remember where he comes from, he don't remember his family, he don't remember the names of his kids. All he thinks about is getting high.

ANON: He must be lonely.

PASCAL: He ain't alone. He's got lots of company.

Other shadows appear. They fill the tunnel. A faint rumbling.

PASCAL: The train's right on time.
ANON: Train? What train?
PASCAL: Come on, Lan. Or whatever your real name is.

PASCAL scrambles up a ladder to a ledge at the top of the tunnel. A bright light approaches.

PASCAL: You stay down there, you're gonna get squashed like a
    pancake. You think I'm foolin, you watch and see.

The rumbling gets louder. The light grows brighter. ANON *hesitates and then scrambles up the ladder. The sound of steel against steel. The roar of a giant engine. A train bears down.* PASCAL *and* ANON *jump onto the roof of a boxcar. And then the train thunders past.*
    Night sky. Stars glitter. The top of the train speeding through the landscape. PASCAL *and* ANON *on top of the box car.*

PASCAL: Listen.

The sound of the train. A percussion of engines and metal. PASCAL *taps out a beat.* ANON *joins him. Their rhythm builds.* PASCAL *stops tapping and looks at* ANON. ANON *notices that* PASCAL *is watching him and stops tapping.*

PASCAL: You know, you kinda look like a monkey.
ANON: I don't look like a monkey.
PASCAL: Yeah you do. Around the chin. And the ears. You have
    monkey ears. What's wrong with monkeys?
ANON: I don't look like a monkey.
PASCAL: Monkeys are good luck. Relax, monkey.

The sound of the train. The landscape speeds by.

ANON: How far does this train go?

PASCAL: Far.

ANON: We could keep going and going.

PASCAL: We could, but we won't. We got a destination.

ANON: Oh yeah? Where's that?

PASCAL: A place I hear we can get some work, make a little money, get set up. Get some new clothes. You, monkey, are in need of new clothes.

ANON: What would you do if you had all the money in the world?

PASCAL: First, I'd buy a brand-new car so I could go anywhere in style. Nice shiny rims, nice sound system so I could listen to my tunes. And then I'd eat all I could eat: steak and french fries and pizza. I love pizza, pepperoni pizza. That's the best. What about you?

ANON: I don't know.

PASCAL: Yeah, you do.

ANON: I don't know. I guess I'd buy my mom a house, you know, a big house with a big yard so she'd never have to worry, so she'd always have a place where she could go. You know, a home.

PASCAL: A home, huh. That's nice. That's cool.

The sound of the train. The landscape speeds by.

PASCAL: Do you believe in fate?

ANON: Like fortune telling?

PASCAL: Kinda. Like everything that happens to you is already decided before you're even born.

ANON: And you don't have a choice?

PASCAL: No choice.

ANON: I don't know. I guess I don't think about stuff like that.

PASCAL: Where I come from, they try to tell your future from the stars.

ANON: Yeah? What do my stars say?

PASCAL: Hmmm. You will travel far. And have a bumpy ride.

ANON: You know what, I knew that already.

PASCAL: The stars don't lie.

ANON: No, they're just telling me what I already know.

PASCAL: Look at them all. So many stars. They look exactly like they do at home.

ANON: You think about home?

PASCAL: Not so much. How about you?

ANON: I think about my mom sometimes.

PASCAL: Yeah? What's she like?

ANON: I don't know how to describe her. Like a mom.

PASCAL: Does she smell like soap?

ANON: Yeah. Like soap and clean clothes and some kind of flower, I don't know what it is.

PASCAL: Does she have a big enormous bag she carries everything in?

ANON: Yeah.

PASCAL: Do her eyes crinkle up when she laughs?

ANON: Uh huh.

PASCAL: Does she sing sometimes when she thinks no one's listening?

ANON: Yeah.

PASCAL: Does she chop vegetables really fast?

ANON: So fast you can't even believe it. Yeah.

PASCAL: Does she sew?

ANON: Uh huh.

PASCAL: And when she sews, the stitches are so tiny and even, and you think how can they be so . . .

ANON: . . . perfect.

PASCAL: Yeah. I think about my mom, too.

ANON: Where's she now?

The sound of the train begins to transform into a menacing rhythm of metal grinding against metal.

ANON: Pascal?

PASCAL: We're almost there.

ANON: Pascal?

The sound of metal grinding against metal grows. It sounds like human voices wailing.

ANON: Pascal, where's your mom? Where is she now?
PASCAL: You know how to jump? You know how to fall? Watch. I'll
    show you.

PASCAL *jumps from the moving train.* ANON *follows.*
    ANON *and* PASCAL *hit the ground. They tumble down a giant hill. The world is a blur. They tumble and roll, coming to a stop in front of a giant steel door. The door is ajar. The sound of opera. A ghostly fluorescent light from within.* ANON *and* PASCAL *enter.* MR. ZYCLO *sits alone in the room. He listens to opera on an old Victrola. He is a butcher in a white coat with a tiny blood stain. He has one eye. He makes sausages with a meat grinder. He is surrounded by packages of frozen meat, raw and shrink-wrapped.* ANON *is transfixed by the packages of meat.*

MR. ZYCLO: A good sausage is one of life's great pleasures.
    (To Pascal.) Do you like sausage? Here. For you.

PASCAL *approaches reluctantly. He eats the sausage.*

MR. ZYCLO: You like that? My secret recipe. Top secret. *(To* ANON.*)*
    How about you? Sausage?
ANON *doesn't move.*

MR. ZYCLO: Don't you like sausage? No? No matter. More for me and
    your friend then.

MR. ZYCLO *eats sausage ravenously.*

PASCAL: We're looking for work.
MR. ZYCLO: What kind of work?

Anon(ymous)   31

PASCAL: Whatever you have.

MR. ZYCLO: Times are tight. As you see, it's just me now. I had to let everyone else go.

PASCAL: We're good workers. We can do anything, anything you need.

ANON (*whispering*): Psst. Pascal. Pascal—

PASCAL: What?

MR. ZYCLO: I could use some help cleaning up. I make a mess, my line of work.

PASCAL: We could do that. How much?

MR. ZYCLO: Trust me. I'll do right by you. What's the matter with your friend? Cat got his tongue?

ANON: What kind of meat is that?

MR. ZYCLO: Brain. It's a delicacy. High in protein. Very rich. Fry it up with a little garlic. Very tasty.

PASCAL: Where do we start?

MR. ZYCLO: There's a bucket and some sponges. I want to you scrub, scrub, scrub. I'll be back.

MR. ZYCLO *exits. At the back of the room, there's another door.* ANON *examines the machine.* PASCAL *starts to clean.* ANON *reaches out to touch the machine.*

ANON: Look at this thing. Look at how sharp it is.

PASCAL: Leave it.

ANON *moves away from the machine. He looks around the room.*

ANON: It's cold.

PASCAL: Don't complain. We earn some money, and then we go.

ANON: How do we know he's gonna pay us?

PASCAL: He'll pay. Before you know it, we'll earn enough money, we can go anywhere. We can do whatever we want.

ANON: I don't like this place.

PASCAL: It's just a job. You think too much.

ANON: Maybe you don't think enough.

PASCAL: Maybe you should shut up.

MR. ZYCLO'S PET BIRD *bursts through the door at the back of the room.*
She wears high-heel shoes. She looks at ANON *and* PASCAL. *She squawks*
and then exits. The click click click of her heels.

ANON: What's in there?

ANON *opens the door. Slabs of meat hang from hooks. Blood drips. The*
opera music grows in volume. MR. ZYCLO *appears. He holds a hatchet. He*
approaches PASCAL *and* ANON *as he speaks.*

MR. ZYCLO: Have you seen my bird? I have a little pet bird. I feed
    her little morsels from my hand. She's very tame. I coo to her
    and she coos back. This is my freezer. It's very cold. Aren't you
    cold? I have to keep it cold like this or else the meat gets bad.
    Look at all this meat. Isn't it strange? When you cut off the
    head and scrape off the skin, when you boil away the fat and the
    gristle, it's hard to tell what something was. Was it a cow? Or a
    pig? Or a goat? Was it a little baby lamb? Or was it something
    else? A different kind of meat? Fleshy and tender and vaguely
    familiar. Do you know what goes into my sausages? Do you know
    what makes them so mouth-wateringly delicious? Do you have
    an idea? The tiniest inkling? What? Cat got your tongue?

MR. ZYCLO *raises the hatchet. Blackout. The sound of the hatchet*
whizzing through the air and then a dull thud as it hits. The sound of the
giant steel door closing. The sound of opera stops. Then the sound of a bird
whistling.

Lights up. The giant steel door to the outside is closed. MR. ZYCLO *is*
making sausages with a meat grinder. Blood is everywhere, on the floor,
on the walls. His white coat is splattered with blood. PASCAL *is gone.*
ANON *watches* MR. ZYCLO. MR. ZYCLO'S PET BIRD *clicks and paces*

frantically. The click click click of her high-heel shoes. She chirps and squawks and caws throughout the scene, trying to speak.

ANON: Where's my friend?

MR. ZYCLO: What friend?

ANON: His name's Pascal and he was here, he was right here just a second ago.

MR. ZYCLO: There's nobody here named Pascal. You must be confused. There's just me and you and my little pet bird.

ANON: He was right here. He was standing right here.

MR. ZYCLO: What was your name again? I don't think you ever said.

ANON: Uh, monkey.

MR. ZYCLO: Monkey. How delightful. You do look a little like a monkey, one of those worried little monkeys you see in the zoo. They look like little old men, nibbling on a piece of fruit, scratching at their fleas, racing around their cage looking for a way out except, of course, there is no way out.

MR. ZYCLO'S PET BIRD *squawks.*

MR. ZYCLO: What a noisy bird. I used to have two, but then one of them, he flew away.

ANON *tries to open the steel door.*

MR. ZYCLO: Now I keep the door shut tight or else she'll fly away, too, and then I'll be all alone.

MR. ZYCLO'S PET BIRD *squawks and caws frantically. A crescendo of squawking.*

MR. ZYCLO: BE QUIET, BIRD, OR I'LL COOK YOU IN A POT. *(To* ANON.*)* How do you like your meat, monkey? Well-done or rare?

ANON *doesn't respond.* MR. ZYCLO *opens a box, takes out a bottle of wine, uncorks it.*

MR. ZYCLO: "Rare, please. I like my meat rare." What about a glass of wine? "O yes please. A glass of wine would be delightful." Only, I have to tell you, I'm a little tired of cabernets. I prefer Chianti. A good Chianti can be just the thing.

MR. ZYCLO'S PET BIRD *chirps frantically to* ANON.

ANON: I, I, I don't know much about wine.

MR. ZYCLO: No?

ANON: No.

MR. ZYCLO: Well why would you? It's just wine.

ANON: I've always wanted to learn.

MR. ZYCLO: Really.

ANON: I just never knew anyone who knew anything about wine. Not like yourself.

MR. ZYCLO: Some people are such snobs about wine. My feeling is, you like what you like. There's no right or wrong. There's only what you like. Here I'll show you.

MR. ZYCLO *pours a little wine in a glass.*

The butcher, Mr. Zyclo (Steve Hendrickson), gives Anon (Michael Ray Escamilla) a lesson in wine appreciation. Photograph by Rob Levine.

MR. ZYCLO: Now here we have a lovely vintage. Full-bodied, robust. Twirl it, see how it streaks, that's what it should do, that's exactly what it should do. And then we sniff. And now we taste. Ah. Oaky.

MR. ZYCLO *finishes the glass, and then he downs the bottle.*

MR. ZYCLO: Fine wine is one of life's great pleasures. It's civilized. We live in nasty, brutish times. I try to remember what it is to be civilized. Linen napkins. Opera. Fine wine. Because it matters. It means something. But sometimes it can be so lonely, it can be so very lonely. You have no idea. It's nice to have someone to share a glass of wine with. I'll miss you when you go.

ANON: Go?

MR. ZYCLO: Thwack. Thwack. Sausage doesn't grow on trees. Sorry, monkey. That's just the way it is. And then it will just be me and my little bird. My little bird keeps me company, but she's sad. She had a little baby bird, but he flew away.

ANON: Maybe if you left the door open, he'd fly back.

MR. ZYCLO: Oh you're very tricky. But if I open the door, you'll run away, my little sausage-to-be.

ANON: Ssh. Listen. I think I hear a bird outside.

MR. ZYCLO *opens the heavy steel door.*

MR. ZYCLO: No bird.

ANON: I swore I heard a bird just now.

MR. ZYCLO'S PET BIRD *chirps.*

ANON: There. Listen.

MR. ZYCLO'S PET BIRD *chirps again.*

MR. ZYCLO: Was that a bird? Cheep? Cheep? Cheep? O I feel so sleepy. So very very sleepy.

MR. ZYCLO *collapses in a drunken stupor.* MR. ZYCLO'S PET BIRD *comes over to Anon. The click click click of her high-heel shoes. She takes her shoe off and gives it to* ANON. ANON *approaches* MR. ZYCLO, *raises the shoe, and smashes it down. He puts out* MR. ZYCLO*'s one good eye with the heel.* MR. ZYCLO *shrieks.*

MR. ZYCLO: My eye! My eye! What have you done to my eye? I can't
     see. I can't see anything. My eye, my eye! It's killing me!

MR. ZYCLO *hears* ANON *and his* PET BIRD.

MR. ZYCLO: Little bird?

MR. ZYCLO *approaches* ANON.

MR. ZYCLO: Little bird? Is that you?

MR. ZYCLO *lunges toward* ANON. ANON *overpowers* MR. ZYCLO *and shoves meat into his mouth.*

ANON: How's that?! How does that taste?! Is it full-bodied?! Is it
     robust, is it civilized enough for you?!

MR. ZYCLO'S PET BIRD *shrieks. Frenzied, she descends on* MR. ZYCLO. *She is all nails and teeth and stiletto heels.* MR. ZYCLO *howls. A chaos of feathers and screeching and blood.* ANON *slips through the giant steel door.*
     ANON *runs. He runs. He runs. The world transforms into a giant freeway. The sound of the interstate like an ocean. Fields of tall grass as far as the eye can see. A wind makes the grass rustle and whisper.* ANON *doubles over, winded, unable to run any further.* IGNACIO *appears through the grass.*

ANON: Hey. Wait. Which way do I go? I don't know which way to go.
     Say something. Why don't you say something?

BELEN *appears behind* ANON. *She holds a small suitcase.*

BELEN: He cannot.

ANON *turns around, startled. He sees* BELEN. *The sound of the tall grass rustling and whispering.*

BELEN: My name is Belen. What's your name?

ANON: Nobody. I'm nobody. Do I know you? I feel like I know you.

BELEN: Maybe from a past life. Do you remember me from a past life?

ANON: I don't remember.

BELEN: When you die, they say you forget. You forget where you come from. You forget the people you love. That's what dying means: to forget. So you have to try very hard to remember. You have to keep what you love right in front of you, like a shiny coin at the bottom of a well.

The sound of NEMASANI *singing.* NEMASANI *appears.* ANON *sees her.*

ANON: I need to get back. I need to find my way back. I need to find my way home.

BELEN: Where's home?

ANON: Faraway.

BELEN: How far?

ANON: Far. Very far.

NEMASANI *fades away. The singing fades away. All that's left is the sound of the tall grass rustling and whispering.* IGNACIO *whispers to* BELEN.

ANON: What's he saying?

BELEN: He says we should go now. He says we'll die if we stay here. He says if we're lucky a truck will come by and we can get a ride. He says I should go with you. He says you'll protect me. (*To* IGNACIO.) Poppa, wait—

BELEN *tries to follow* IGNACIO, *but she can't. He walks away into the tall grass without looking back. The wind murmurs.* BELEN *and* ANON *watch as* IGNACIO *disappears.*

ANON: Why doesn't he come with us now?

BELEN: He would, if he could.

ANON: Why can't he?

BELEN: When my father left our village, he promised to come back and get me. He never made it. He died on his way back. Don't you see? My father is a ghost.

The wind picks up. A howling wind. A truck thunders by. Headlights. The sound of brakes.

    The cab of a truck speeding down the freeway. STRYGAL *drives.* BELEN *sits between* ANON *and* STRYGAL. *The inside of the truck is hot. The faint sound of tapping.*

STRYGAL: Hot enough for ya? Oooh boy is it hot. Never used to be this hot. It's the ozone. The ozone's all messed up. So where you kids headed to?

ANON: Home.

STRYGAL: Home sweet home. That's nice. So where's home? Far away is what I'm guessing. What's the matter? Cat got your tongue?

ANON: What did you say?

STRYGAL: What? Cat got your tongue? Ah, it's just a thing my dad used to say.

ANON: Your dad? Who was your dad?

STRYGAL: Why do you care? He wasn't nobody. He was just a mean old drunk. Owned a butcher shop out in the boonies. Had one good eye. Can you believe it? Liked to listen to opera. If there's one thing I can't stand it's opera. I hate opera. *(To* BELEN.*)* Whaddya got in that suitcase, girly girl? Diamonds? Rubies? State secrets?

STRYGAL *reaches over to touch* BELEN.

ANON: Hey.

STRYGAL: Relax, pal. Relax. I was just picking some lint off the little lady's dress, just a little piece of fuzz. Hot, huh? It must be over a hundred. I'm sweatin like a pig.

The sound of tapping grows.

ANON: What's that sound?

STRYGAL: Could be the muffler.

ANON: What's in back? What are you hauling?

STRYGAL: This and that. It's a cash business. I don't ask a lot of questions.

ANON: I can hear something. There.

STRYGAL: Word to the wise, pal: keep your nose out of where it don't belong.

ANON: I think we should stop. I think we should stop and check.

STRYGAL: Look, I already stopped for you and your little friend here, out of the goodness of my heart. I'm not stopping anymore. I'm already running late. *(To* BELEN.*)* Anybody ever tell you, you're very pretty. You got very pretty hair.

The sound of tapping is joined by the distant sound of murmuring voices.

STRYGAL: This clown, he's not your boyfriend, is he? He can't be. You're too young to have a boyfriend. You're real quiet, ain't you? I like that. I can't stand girls who yak and yak and can't shut up. I like quiet girls. You speak English? I'll teach you how to speak English.

ANON: Listen. There right there. Somebody's back there. Who's back there?

STRYGAL: Nobody.

ANON: There's people back there. I can hear them. How many people are back there?

STRYGAL: That's none of your business, pal.

ANON: It's too hot. They'll suffocate. Stop the truck.

STRYGAL: You gotta be kidding me.

ANON: I said stop the truck. Pull over.

STRYGAL: No.

ANON *grabs the wheel.* ANON *and* STRYGAL *struggle for control of the wheel.*

STRYGAL: What're you doing? Are you outta your mind?

BELEN: Stop—

ANON: Pull over—

STRYGAL: No—

BELEN: What are you doing?

ANON: I said pull over—

STRYGAL: Are you insane—

BELEN: Wait—

The blare of a horn. Bright light fills the cab of the truck. Crash. Darkness.
Darkness. Inside the back of STRYGAL's *truck.* CHORUS OF REFUGEES
in the darkness.

CHORUS:

My name was Maria	I came to America on a ship.
My name was Ahmet	I came to America in a truck.
My name was Soo Chai	I walked a thousand miles.
My name was Roberto	I crossed a giant desert.
My name was Farid	It was so hot I couldn't breathe.
My name was Aram	It was so cold, my fingers froze.
My name was Yelena	I traveled in the night.
My name was Tiang	I always traveled in the night.
My name was Maricella	I was afraid.
My name was Sanjit	I made no sound.
My name was Pran	I was invisible.
My name was Malik	I was like the murmuring wind.
My name was Jiang Tsu	I was the edge of a shadow.
My name was Fatima	I was flicker out of the corner of your eye.

My name was Yousif	I came here to make a better life.
My name was Duc	I had so many hopes.
My name was Saiid	I had so many dreams.
My name was Chia	But I died.
My name was Miguel	I died.
My name was Trinh	I died along the way.
My name was Faisal	Please tell my sister.
My name was Meena	Tell my brother.
My name was Abraham	Tell my father.
My name was Song	Tell my mother.
My name was Joseph	Tell my son.
My name was Alicia	Tell my daughter.
Remember me	Remember me.
Remember me	

A howling wind. The sound of metal doors being pushed open. The CHORUS OF REFUGEES *spill out from the darkness. They are ghosts. They disperse. A howling wind.* ANON *emerges from the wreckage, cut and bleeding.*

A city. Night. The sounds of traffic. A pay phone ringing. The sounds of transistor radios playing songs from Southeast Asia and the Middle East. A fragment of a telenovela on the TV. The sound of street vendors. A distant siren. A door appears. ANON *goes through the door. He is inside a dive bar. Dim reddish light. Ancient cigarette smoke. Mirrors. A juke box plays an old song.* SERZA *wipes down the bar. The* LONE BARFLY *dances.*

SERZA: Well, look at what the cat dragged in. Welcome to the last stop, stranger, the end of the road, rock bottom. Come on in. Make yourself at home. We're all friends here. The more the merrier, right?

The LONE BARFLY *snorts.*

ANON: Water. Please. Can I have a glass of water?

SERZA *pours him a glass of water.* ANON *begins to drink.*

SERZA: I gotta charge you for that, sugar. You know that, right?

ANON: I don't have any money.

SERZA: No money? You come in here and ask me for a drink and you
  don't have any money? What? Does it look like I'm running
  some kind of charity? Is that what it looks like to you? *(To the*
  LONE BARFLY.*)* He thinks I'm running a charity.

The LONE BARFLY *snorts.* ANON *pushes the half-drunk glass of water back
across the bar.*

SERZA: Never mind, take it. Just take it.

ANON *drinks.* SERZA *studies him.*

SERZA: What happened to you? You get in a fight?

ANON: No. It wasn't like that.

SERZA: What was it like?

ANON: I don't want to talk about it.

SERZA: You got someplace to go?

ANON: No.

SERZA: You're just a kid. You should go home. Just go on home.

ANON: I don't have a home. I don't have a family. I don't have that. I
  don't have anyone.

ANON *starts to exit and stumbles.*

SERZA: Hey, hey, hey. It's OK. It's all right.

SERZA *cleans off the blood from the side of* ANON's *face.* ANON *lets her. The
song on the jukebox plays.*

ANON: It hurts. It's like all these bad things keep happening and I
  can't stop them. It's like everyone I get close to, they all go away.
  It's like they all go away and there's nothing I can do.

The song on the jukebox plays.

SERZA: Ssssh. You're getting yourself all worked up. You gotta let it go. You gotta just let it go. *(Beat.)* Dance with me. Why don't you dance with me?

The song on the jukebox plays. ANON *and* SERZA *begin to dance. The* LONE BARFLY *dances.* ANON *begins to pull away.*

ANON: I gotta go.
SERZA: You don't want to go. Just stay. Stay a while. You can stay here as long you want. You can stay here forever.

ANON *struggles to get out of* SERZA's *bar. A mist rolls in. Sheets and sheets of billowing fog. The bar slowly fills with fog. The song on the jukebox begins to distort.* ANON *sees* IGNACIO *walking away. He pulls away from* SERZA *and approaches* IGNACIO. SERZA *recedes from view.*
   The world is engulfed in fog. The distant sound of war. IGNACIO *is walking away.* ANON *tries to catch up with him, but he can't.*

ANON: Hey! Wait! Wait, come back!

IGNACIO *vanishes.* STRYGAL *appears. Ghostly white. He clutches the steering wheel of his truck.*

ANON: Hey! I want to talk to you. Hey!

STRYGAL *vanishes.* BELEN *appears. She's holding her suitcase.*

ANON: Belen? Belen, is that you?

BELEN *turns around.* ANON *sees her dress is red with blood.*

ANON: Belen, wait.

BELEN *starts walking away.* ANON *tries to follow her, but he can't keep up. He loses her. The sound of war.* PASCAL *appears.*

PASCAL: Where I come from, soldiers came to my village. I saw them coming, and I ran into the forest. I hid beneath the leaves. I was so still. I could hear everything. I could hear the sound of fire and men shouting. I could hear my little brother. I could hear him crying and my mother saying don't cry, don't cry. I could hear the machetes. I could hear their screams. And then it was quiet. It was so quiet. All I could hear was the sound of my heart beating. Will you remember me?

ANON: Pascal?

PASCAL: When you're old and you look back, will you remember me? Will you remember a friend who died long ago?

PASCAL *recedes from view.*

ANON: Pascal? Pascal, wait!

CHORUS: I disappeared.
                I became invisible.
                I ran away.
                I escaped.
                I shed my skin.
                I changed my name.
                I became anonymous.
                My name is anonymous.
                My name is anonymous.
                My name is anonymous.
ANON: My name is anonymous.
                My name is anonymous.

The sounds of war grow closer. The CHORUS OF REFUGEES *disperses in all different directions. The whistling of bombs falling from the sky. They get closer.* ANON *hears a woman singing a fragment of a familiar song.*

NEMASANI *becomes visible. She sings.* ANON *begins to go toward her. The sound of a bomb falling.* NAJA *appears and pulls* ANON *out of the path of the explosion. The world shatters. Brilliant light. Dust motes swirling in the light. Then darkness.*

ANON *is alone in the darkness.*

ANON: There was a war, and me and my mom, we escaped on a boat. And then there was a storm, and the boat we were on sank, and lots of people drowned. I know this for a fact. And later I was in a refugee camp. And then later I was adopted by a nice American family. These are facts.

Light on NICE AMERICAN FAMILY *posing for a photograph. The father is played by the actor playing* SENATOR LAIUS, *the mother is played by the actor playing* HELEN LAIUS, *and the daughter is played by the actor playing* CALISTA.

ANON: They lived in a fancy house full of so many things. But they weren't my family, and it wasn't my home. And I ran away. That's a fact, too. These are all facts. But facts are only part of the story.

Camera flash. The NICE AMERICAN FAMILY *recedes from view.*

Light up on RITU, ALI, *and* NASREEN *in the kitchen of an Indian restaurant.*

ANON: I think that your life is made up of all these bits and pieces. And sometimes the pieces don't fit together. There's a piece that's missing. And you try to fill in the blanks, you try to remember, and sometimes you can see a shape of something you can almost make out, you can almost see a face—
RITU: Your mother's face.
ANON: Yes.
RITU: There's a place I know. On the other side of town. I worked there when we first came to this country. I sewed clothes: blue jeans, T-shirts. It was a terrible place.

ALI: It was a sweatshop. They should've shut it down years ago. All those women from all those different countries. So many women from all over the world. Ah, Ritu—

RITU: Yes, Ali. Yes.

ANON: What are you saying?

RITU: It's a small world, stranger, smaller than you think.

ANON: You think my mother—? That's crazy.

RITU: Is it?

ANON: What are the chances? One in a million?

RITU: What do you have to lose? There's no way to know unless you go and see. You've come this far. Trust me. I have an idea. Nasreen, put the rice on. Ali, get the ghee. (*To* ANON.) Now listen to me, listen carefully.

Ritu explains her plan to ANON. NASREEN *and* ALI *begin to prepare food. The sound of cooking. The chopping of vegetables. Running water. Bursts of flame. The sound of sizzling and bubbling. The sound of creation. The kitchen fills with steam.*

The kitchen transforms into the sewing factory. The SEWING LADIES *sew. The sound of the sewing machines.* MR. YURI MACKUS *strides toward* NEMASANI. SEWING LADY 2 *follows him.*

MR. MACKUS (*to* NEMASANI): LIES LIES LIES! I've had it with your lies! I'm on to you. You tell me you're going to marry me when this shroud is done, but it's never going to be done, is it? Is it? Because you undo it in the night when no one's looking—except for Vanna here who happened to see what you were up to and had the decency to tell me. Thank you, Vanna. As for you, you deceitful, duplicitous, mendacious minx, your little charade is over. We're getting married now. No more stalling! No more delays!

Enter ANON *with Indian takeout.*

MR. MACKUS: Who are you? What do you want? Why are you here?

ANON: Somebody ordered takeout.

MR. MACKUS: Who? Not me. I didn't order any takeout. I've already eaten. And they don't eat. Not when I eat. I don't know when they eat. That's not my concern. Why am I telling you this? Why am I even talking to you? I don't have to explain myself.

NEMASANI *starts to exit.*

MR. MACKUS: Where do you think you're going? We have things to do. We're getting married. And then we're going to live HAPPILY EVER AFTER! HAPPY HAPPY HAPPY! THE END!

ANON: Leave her alone.

MR. MACKUS: What did you say?

ANON: You heard me.

MR. MACKUS: Is someone talking? I think it must be a little fly is buzzing around my head. It's not a fly. It's you. And who are you again? I'll tell you who you are. You're nobody. You're a tiny cockroach I squash with my hand. You're a piece of lint I flick off my jacket. You're chewing gum on the bottom of my shoe. You're faceless and nameless. You're a dime a dozen, people like you.

NEMASANI *tries to get free of* MR. MACKUS.

MR. MACKUS: Stop it! Be still!

NEMASANI: You're hurting me.

MR. MACKUS: Be still!

ANON: Leave her alone.

MR. MACKUS: Leave her alone. You want me to leave her alone. That's funny. You're funny. You're a funny funny guy.

MR. MACKUS *draws a sword.*

MR. MACKUS: Make me, little fly.

NAJA *appears. She throws a sword to* ANON.

ANON: OK. If you insist.

ANON and MR. MACKUS *battle like ancient warriors. An aerial, acrobatic battle. They twist and tumble and kick. They use pieces of the sewing factory—spindles and scissors and bolts of cloth and spools of colored thread. The sound of slashing. A chaos of cloth. A tangle of thread.* ANON *corners* MR. MACKUS.

MR. MACKUS: Oh, please don't kill me, don't kill me, please don't kill me—what was your name, stranger? Friend? I don't think I caught it.
ANON: Call me anonymous.

ANON cuts a single thread with his sword. A ton of clothes rain down from the ceiling. MR. MACKUS *is buried in an avalanche of clothes.* NAJA *pushes open an exit door. A wind blows in from the outdoors. The sound of voices carried on the wind, echoes. The* CHORUS OF REFUGEES *echoes what came before.*

CHORUS: Where I come from is far away from here—
        is oxen in rice field—
        is hills the color of green tea—
        is jungles filled with jaguars—
        and pythons thick as a grown man's thigh—
        is poison frogs the size of a thumbnail—
        and squirrels that can fly from tree to tree—
        is waterfalls taller than the tallest skyscraper—
        is olive trees and ancient desert—
        is sampans and temple bells—
        is sandstorms—
        and monsoon rains—
        is tapir and okapi—
        and electric blue butterflies with wings as wide as
           my arms—

NEMASANI's *shroud transforms into a butterfly and flies away.*

The rooftop of the sewing factory. Sunset. The sky is fuchsia and tangerine and indigo blue. ANON *and* NEMASANI *are alone.*

NEMASANI: Where I come from, there are butterflies like nothing you've ever seen.

ANON: Blue.

NEMASANI: Yes, blue so blue.

ANON: With huge wings.

NEMASANI: Huge.

ANON *(spreading his arms)*: Like this. Bigger even.

NEMASANI: Yes. *(Recognizing something in* ANON.*)* Yes.

ANON: I remember.

NEMASANI *and* ANON *look at each other.*

ANON: What if I told you . . . ?

NEMASANI: No. Don't say it—

ANON: What if somehow—

NEMASANI: Please don't—

ANON: But what if—

NEMASANI: I don't believe in "what if." "What if" will break your heart.

ANON: You have a son—

NEMASANI: My son died. He died a long time ago. He was just a little boy and he died.

ANON: What if he didn't?

NEMASANI: Stop—

ANON: What if he survived?

NEMASANI: I said stop—

ANON: Please listen to me—

NEMASANI: No. No. I can't. I'm sorry. I'm so sorry.

NEMASANI *begins to exit.*

ANON: What do you remember?
          Because what I remember, what I remember is you.
          How you used to hold me.
          You held me and you sang to me.
          I remember the song you sang to me.

Somewhere in the night, the sound of a woman singing an ancient song.

NEMASANI: How can I know you are who you say you are?
ANON: I'll tell you the story of my life and then you can decide.
          It begins in the middle.
          On the border.
          On the crossing.
          It begins in the place in between.

The song continues. NEMASANI *approaches* ANON. *The sounds of the city begin to filter through and fuse with the ancient song. They make a new song. It grows like a beautiful hybrid bloom in the wilderness.*

END OF PLAY

THE LOST BOYS OF SUDAN

Lonnie Carter

The world premier of *The Lost Boys of Sudan* was directed by Peter Brosius and opened on March 27, 2007, at Children's Theatre Company. *The Lost Boys of Sudan* was developed with the support of The Playwright's Center and through Playground, a collaboration between Children's Theatre Company and New Dramatists. *The Lost Boys of Sudan* was made possible in part by grants from Theatre Communications Group/Met Life Foundation Extended Collaboration program, The Andrew W. Mellon Foundation, and the Jerome Foundation in celebration of the Jerome Hill Centennial and in recognition of the valuable cultural contributions of artists to society.

CREATIVE TEAM

Scenic design: Debra Booth

Costume design: Helen Q. Huang

Lighting design: Geoff Korf

Composition and sound design: Andre Pluess

Dramaturgy: Elissa Adams

Stage manager: Jenny R. Friend

Assistant stage manager: Jody Gavin

Stage management intern: Annelise Castleberry

CAST

K-GAR OLLIE, a Dinka Boy	Samuel G. Roberson Jr.
A. I. JOSH, a Dinka Boy	André Samples
T-MAC SAM, a Dinka Boy	Namir Smallwood
MOLLY MIDNIGHT	Nadia Hulett
COPERNICUS, CRISPUS ATTUCKS	Shawn Hamilton

MOIRA MIDNIGHT	Annie Enneking
NYANDIER, K-GAR'S MOTHER	Marvette Knight
KOOKOOROOKU, RUMMY	Ashford J. Thomas
JUSTICE MINISTER, CLAYTON POWELL, BASKETBALL COACH	James A. Williams

ENSEMBLE: Nadia Hulett, Shawn Hamilton, Annie Enneking, Marvette Knight, Ashford J. Thomas, and James A. Williams

UNDERSTUDIES: Kelsie Jepsen, Celeste Jones

CHARACTERS (in order of appearance)

A CHORUS OF CATTLE, wanting to be herded, wanting to be heard

AYOUN, the prima inter pares

THE BOYS OF THE DINKA TRIBE, a Chorus

A. I. JOSH, a Dinka Boy

T-MAC SAM, a Dinka Boy

K-GAR OLLIE, a Dinka Boy

K-GAR OLLIE'S MOTHER

A. I. JOSH'S FATHER

TWELVE, a wizened twelve-year-old warlord

FIRST FEMALE BODYGUARD

SECOND FEMALE BODYGUARD

CHRISTIAN WARLORD

MUSLIM WARLORD

GUERRILLA

KRYPTO ARMY MEMBER

CRAZED BOY RADIO OPERATOR

COPERNICUS PTOLEMY PATRICK, Headmaster at Camp Kakuma

A CHORUS OF ELDERS

MIRIAM MAKER, administrator of Camp Kakuma

JUSTICE MINISTER

NYANDIER

CRISPUS ATTUCKS, a driver in Fargo, North Dakota

CLAYTON POWELL, works for Social Reach

MOIRA MIDNIGHT, Student Placement Counselor

MOLLY MIDNIGHT, high school student and daughter of
    Moira Midnight

RUMMY, an American high school student

BASKETBALL COACH

KOOKOOROOKU, a Dinka Boy

PLACE: The Sudan and points in all directions, including Fargo,
    North Dakota

TIME: Sadly, The Eternal Present

╫╫

ACT ONE

Our CHORUS, *a Herd of Cattle wanting to be herded, wanting to be heard.*

CHORUS: We are the Cattle of the Sudan
            We are proud four-footed creatures
            Dinka Boys of Dinka tribe tend our herds
            Where and all they can
            They are students, we are teachers
            This is our school, out in this bush
            Where boys learn to be men
            We are the rule, here in this bush
            For boys twelve, even eight and ten
            At night ourselves are sides, our sides are pillows
            We cattle rest a little in the dark, under weeping willows
            We hear the sound of insects whirring, lions purring,
            Hyenas laughing at us loudly
            We're all a little frightened, in and out of sleep,
            But still we're feeling, feeling proudly
            At dawn we move—they move us—after we've moved
                them awake
            We scatter birds, all types of fowl, even wildebeests

We look out for the cheetahs, eyeing us, so many feasts
We have our favorite faves, we cannot hide that
These boys, each and every one,
Is precious to us
These three called A. I., T-Mac, K-Gar
We put them forth as best; it isn't fair
Perhaps, but each one, lovely, always tries
To soothe our limbs and horns and stroke each hide
And make us feel like we're the only one
A. I. Josh, T-Mac Samuel, K-Gar Oliver

Sonja Parks *(left)*, Ashford J. Thomas *(center)*, Nadia Hulett *(right)*, and the rest of the cast introduce the audience to their home, a village in Sudan, during the world premiere of *The Lost Boys of Sudan* (2007). Photograph by Rob Levine.

A . I . JOSH, *discovered with his favorite cow,* AYOUN.

A . I . JOSH: Ayoun, my precious cow. You know today I am a man.
But how I know this when I can barely shave. I've passed this
dozen years, I know I can take care of you. And now we're out
here in this bush alone with twenty other boys and cows who're
theirs. We're all, each tested, each is on his own. We're not alone,
we're each of us in pairs. We face the days, the nights, we're
joined as one. Ayoun, Ayoun, together we aren't none.

A . I . JOSH *falls asleep at the edge of his village on the side of* AYOUN.

T-MAC SAM: I don't want to. I don't want to. I won't go into the Bush.
I don't want to grow up as they say I must. I don't care about
cows. Why don't they walk on their back legs as I do? In all the
generations they never heard a boy about to be a man. Once utter
a complaint about going to the Bush? Hooray for them! I set the
record. Yes, I love our cows, but they will understand. Neither of
us, my personal cow or me, if we stay here, will be the slightest
bit disappointed. The Bush be damned!

K-GAR OLLIE, *with his mother.*

K-GAR OLLIE: Mother, I'm off to the Bush. Mother, how can you hold
me back. Mother, know I am duty-bound. I can't stay here
forever, Ma. You should be glad I'm doing what boys must do.
I would never do a thing to hurt you. I would never leave you
alone—you'll be alright. Yes, I have my cow. Mother, now I'm off
to the Bush. Mother, how can you hold me back?

The CHORUS OF CATTLE *appears.*

CHORUS: We have a premonition—we see our boys so bled-dead-
                 tired
            sleep-walking day after day

They cannot move another foot
Their arms have fallen away
The Boys the Dinka Boys find us water, keep us safe
But safety's less and less these days, alas
Men are getting angry and anger doesn't pass
All of them are warriors, who worship different gods
The ones of North fight ones of South
A battle scream pours from each mouth
Children everywhere they threaten
We cows and bulls are frightened
We need some gentle pettin'
Everyone's got bad gripes and awful fears
No one says, "I'm sorry," babies are in tears
Now what's the word we're looking for
When there is civil war
What will happen to us?
If these boys no longer tend us?

A. I. JOSH *asleep on the side of* AYOUN. *His Father approaches and speaks over him.*

FATHER: My son, I have been given a choice. The rebels say you have betrayed them to the government. They say I must kill you or they will kill our entire family. They will not kill you. They say I must do the deed, kill my son, and break the cycle of violence. I do not understand how this breaks the cycle.

He pulls a knife. He hesitates and falls. His falling wakes A. I. JOSH.

A. I. JOSH: Father—

TWELVE, *a wizened twelve-year-old, flanked by two young women in paratrooper uniforms, appears.*

TWELVE: I am Twelve, here to protect you. Just twelve years old, but this gun makes me bold. He was about to kill you, little one. He

had his orders, and not with a gun. But with this knife he would
have slit your throat. As if you were some sacrificial goat.

A. I. JOSH: My father wouldn't raise his hand to me. He's raising me
to head the family

TWELVE: Little Man. Slit your father's throat. He's now the sacrificial
goat.

A. I. JOSH: No. He cannot die.

TWELVE: No matter, the deed is done. You told the government, on
the run. That Twelve would be moving south. Now Twelve's here
to smash your mouth.

FIRST FEMALE BODYGUARD: But Twelve-Year-Old Dear Leader, we
were moving north.

A. I. JOSH: I never spoke to anyone.

SECOND FEMALE BODYGUARD: Dear Leader, this isn't the one who
came forth.

TWELVE: What—

A. I. JOSH: Now I'm the father, no longer the son. What are you
going to do?

TWELVE: Teach you a bloody lesson. Torch your huts. Waste your
herds. Kill your girls. Emasculate your boys. Leave your
skeletons for somebody's toys. Leave your parents for vulture
birds. Blow your village all to bits. We are the Revolution. The
Twelve-Year-Old Solution. (To his BODYGUARDS.) Right, my
honies? You my sisterly twins? Let's hear it for Twelve! Twelve
wins! Twelve wins! Twelve wins!

FIRST BODYGUARD: Twelve loses.

SECOND BODYGUARD: We are the Revolution.

Explosion. Firestorm. Conflagration of village. Enter on steed, a
CHRISTIAN WARLORD. *Speaks to* T-MAC SAM.

WARLORD: This village is being swept of Muslim scum. We all know
where they come from.

T-MAC SAM: I want no part of your god or his fire. I understand
nothing of your desire.

Suddenly the Elephant Rampage has found them. Gunshots. T-MAC
SAM *and the* CHRISTIAN WARLORD *are swept along.* K-GAR OLLIE *sees
someone seize his* MOTHER.

K-GAR OLLIE: Get away from her. You—I don't care who you are.
Keep away from my mother.

We see a man about to rape K-GAR OLLIE'S MOTHER *when suddenly
another man rides in on a camel and beheads the first man. A* MUSLIM
WARLORD *appears on his camel, the dangling head in its mouth.
The* CHRISTIAN WARLORD *crawls onstage.*

CHRISTIAN WARLORD: Muslim Scum.
MUSLIM WARLORD: Christian Swine.
CHRISTIAN: Muslim Toad.
MUSLIM: Christian Slug.
CHRISTIAN: Muslim Bug.
MUSLIM: Christian toad.
CHRISTIAN: Muslim Mine.

K-GAR OLLIE *moves to bring* CHRISTIAN WARLORD *water.*

MUSLIM: I will gladly die for GoodGodGodGood
CHRISTIAN: This is Blasphemy. Mortal Sin. Six thousand times and
more. You'll rot in Hell. There's more war in store.
MUSLIM: I know you, Christian Warlord. Leave our soil, or we'll boil
you, Infidel, for food. In sixty-dollar-a-barrel oil crude.
K-GAR OLLIE: I don't want either of you. Neither of your cutting
ways. You won't assault me nor my mother.

K-GAR OLLIE'S MOTHER *appears.*

MOTHER: We'll fight you and fight you, 'til there's no other of you. If
you know what's good for you, you'll climb upon your camel's
hump. And rumped together, from this trouble you'll bump.

BOTH WARLORDS: Climb, rump, bump together?—He's an infidel!

K-GAR OLLIE: Mother, now's our chance. Leave these cutters, slashers, killers of each other.

K-GAR OLLIE *and* MOTHER *make their escape. The* CHORUS OF CATTLE *appears.*

CHORUS: As young as seven, old as seventeen. Are forced to fight—here there, this side or that. You Dinka, flee!—the word we're looking for. We're just cattle, ever thin, never fat. You've learned our ways, we've had our silent joys. When it was sleep time on us you would lean. It's time for us to low as you lie low.

The BOYS, *bone-weary and starving, come to a stream, where they drink— and cough and sputter.*

A. I. JOSH: Not so fast—or we'll have no fate to seize. I've been thinking—

T-MAC SAM: And not eating, o please—

K-GAR OLLIE: I've been thinking too, and I'd like to know why we—

A. I. JOSH: —don't set up camp beside some stream and stay—

T-MAC SAM: —and try to grow some food and have a life—

K-GAR OLLIE: —it's not too much to ask or is it now? What tribe are you?

T-MAC SAM: And what's your religion?

A. I. JOSH: What does it matter? I'm from the Upper Country. I have my gods.

T-MAC SAM: And so do I. My gods are from the Middle Country, where I am from.

K-GAR OLLIE: I have a god whose face I keep around my neck.

T-MAC SAM: I don't see your god.

K-GAR OLLIE: Around my neck.

A. I. JOSH: I don't see your god.

K-GAR OLLIE *(feeling at his neck)*: My god is gone.

A. I. JOSH: I keep my god in my heart.

K-GAR OLLIE: I don't see your god.

A. I. JOSH: That's because he's inside me.

T-MAC SAM: I want to see your god.

A. I. JOSH: I feel my god.

K-GAR OLLIE: Let me feel him.

A. I. JOSH: I can't just let you feel inside me.

K-GAR OLLIE: You could see and feel my god—if I still had him.

A. I. JOSH: I can't just open myself up.

T-MAC AND K-GAR: Why not?

A. I. JOSH: Because my god doesn't like to be looked at.

K-GAR OLLIE: My god likes—liked—to be looked at all times. I
    wonder who's looking at him now.

K-GAR OLLIE *is having a tough time.*

K-GAR OLLIE: What tribe are you?

A. I. AND T-MAC: Dinka.

K-GAR OLLIE: Dinka?

A. I. JOSH: Yes.

T-MAC SAM: Yes.

K-GAR OLLIE: You speak a little—strange.

A. I. JOSH: What's strange?

T-MAC SAM: Strange?

K-GAR OLLIE: I am Dinka.

A. I. AND T-MAC: You are Dinka?

A. I. JOSH: You speak—

T-MAC SAM: Strange.

A. I. JOSH: If we are all Dinka, we must be from different parts—that
    is why we speak differently, one from the other.

K-GAR OLLIE: But then we all have the same gods. So your god inside
    is my god on my neck. So you don't have to see him, because
    YOU SEE HIM—That is, around your neck. And I can see him too.
    And feel him because he's inside.

T-MAC SAM: Who's my god? I thought I knew. He's in the sky behind
    that cloud. Are you sure we're all Dinka? I know I am—Middle
    Country.

K-GAR OLLIE: Lower Country.

A. I. JOSH: Upper Country.

BOYS: AND ALL DINKA!

A. I. JOSH: I've been thinking—

K-GAR OLLIE: I've been thinking too, and I'd like to know why we . . .

A. I. JOSH: . . . don't set up camp beside some stream and stay . . .

T-MAC SAM: . . . and try to grow some food and have a life . . .

K-GAR OLLIE: . . . it's not too much to ask or is it now?

A. I. JOSH: No, it's not. It's just what we must be doing. Upper, Middle, Lower . . .

K-GAR OLLIE: . . . join together

T-MAC SAM: With gods inside out and outside in and behind—that cloud is gone.

A. I. JOSH: There are some fish in this stream and I'm going to catch me one.

K-GAR OLLIE: Catch and cook.

T-MAC SAM: Or eat one now.

K-GAR OLLIE: Raw fish? You Middle Country Dinkas—

A. I. JOSH: Ayoun—

Other cows drift on.

T-MAC SAM *(referring to his cow)*: This is my god too.

K-GAR OLLIE: And mine. Who will wear ME around HER neck.

A. I. JOSH: I'm seizing a fish.

K-GAR OLLIE: Dinner will be served!

T-MAC SAM: AHA!

A. I. JOSH: It's not too much to ask now, is it? To make—to have a life?

As the BOYS exult and dance, AYOUN steps forward.

AYOUN: I am taking it right down to you and speaking from
                  my heart.
           These Boys are only beginning a journey—this is
                  the start

There is a camp called Camp Kakuma
And there there's a measure of Peace.
It's for boys like ours
But it will take thousands, millions of steps to get there.

Tracer fire. An all-out attack.

RELIEF WORKERS: We are your friends. We're gonna put you to work.
We're here to take you to the oil fields. We're here to assist you.
What are your names? What are your names and whom are you
protecting while we are protecting you?

A. I. JOSH: I am—this is my cow—Ayoun, and I am protecting her.
Ayoun—I—

RELIEF WORKERS: A. I., are you—speak up, OK?

A. I. JOSH (*terrified*): A. I.??—Ayoun—we are one—who are you
protecting us from?

RELIEF WORKERS: Enemies of the State—

A. I. JOSH: The State—of what?

RELIEF WORKERS: The State of the State—you, second boy, what is
your name?

T-MAC SAM: Don't—Don'—Don'—T-t-t-t-t—Smack me—T—Smack
me—don't smack me!

RELIEF WORKERS: We won't hurt you, smack you upside the head.
Not a chance, we'd rather leave our own selves for dead. Trust
us, we bring you relief, keep you out of harm's way. What you get
in return, a spot of work in the oil fields, it's almost like play. So,
T-Mac, we never 'mack you. And you, Third Boy, who are you
and what is your name, OK?

K-GAR OLLIE: OK, K—K-k-k-k-k—

RELIEF WORKERS: K? Great. K-Great, we'll call you K-Great Oliver,
my uncle's middle. We really must bring you into the modern
world. Forward, march!

Time has passed. The BOYS *have marched for several hours. The*
RELIEF WORKERS *are high and drunk. They sing.*

RELIEF WORKERS: *Yes, my lads, a spot of rum n' runnin'*
To the Pump
What could be better, shootin' n' funnin'
To the Pump
Let's hear it for the oil from the soil, let's not be late!
Here we are—At the fields.
On to the Pump
You set the drills below the earth
The oil pours forth for all it's worth
And on to the pump
We'll pay you at the pump
And you'll pay us at the pump.

The oil wells burst forth and drench our heroes.

RELIEF WORKERS: *Yes, we're here, we're so here in the land of Oil*
Sticky wet from boiling soil
Pump away
Pump away
Pump away
Gasoline
O, I wish I were in the land of Oil
Sticky wet from boiling soil
O what fun, pump away
Pump away, Gasoline
So We pump away our life blood
The earth is dry dust and caked mud
We must not die/yes we are/yes we are/yes we must
Pump away
Yes we must
Pump away
Pump away
Gasoline.

The oil wells are set on fire.

BOYS: We are the Boys of Dinka Tribe. We now set forth for Camp
    Kakuma. A camp with a measure of peace. A camp of peace not
    quite without cease.

A. I. JOSH: The shortest march will get us to Kakuma.

T-MAC SAM: I'm not so sure the walk will be so short.

K-GAR OLLIE: If only we had our cattle.

A. I. JOSH: We have to leave—they're soldiers over there!

T-MAC SAM: We follow paths we've many times before.

K-GAR OLLIE: With herds we've grown to love—now where's their
    touch?

BOYS: O, Josh—O, Sam—O, Ollie, is it doom?

A. I. JOSH: Have we found ourselves without support?

T-MAC SAM: Our cattle were our strongest comfort—so

K-GAR OLLIE: We'll never see them more—it's just not fair.

A. I. JOSH: They told us we must go, but what's it for?

T-MAC SAM: They're sure they didn't want us o so much?

K-GAR OLLIE: O, Josh, O, Sam, O, Ollie, what we've done.

BOYS: Is cut our ties to youth to face the gun.

Gunfire. A GUERRILLA SOLDIER *appears.*

GUERRILLA: Hey, mes garçons, you're just the ticket, Oui!
              To fight the South you need the North so bads
              Protection's what we offer you, mais oui, you see?
              We need you much as you need us too, lads
              Please take these guns and pump them up like this
              Get set to shoot when I tell you to
              The enemy is everywhere, snakes hiss
              Snakes always take the form of South'ners too
              Now leave your older ways, we'll show you fame
              You've never had such glory, that's the name
              Of what we're fighting for, it's why we chance
              Just ev'rything, we've nothing but this dance

T-MAC SAM *takes the offered gun.*

T-MAC SAM: Let me see this—what's it called?

GUERRILLA: AK-47, or Kalashnikov.

T-MAC SAM: How you pump it—just like this?

GUERRILLA: You feel it and now you're better off.

T-MAC SAM: I'll join and so will my new brothers.

K-GAR OLLIE: No, I won't. It's crazy, T-Mac Sam.

T-MAC SAM: Feel it, it gives you power.

A. I. AND K-GAR: Over what?

T-MAC SAM: Over this.

GUERRILLA: A little joke, little man, you'll make a good Guerrilla.

T-MAC SAM: No joke, it's already pumped. AK or Kalish, run now, big man has been dumped.

K-GAR OLLIE: We'll join our brother now.

A. I. JOSH: Go—Rilla, boom boom POW.

GUERRILLA *rushes off.*

K-GAR OLLIE: T-Mac, that was great.

A. I. JOSH: Really good, T.

T-MAC SAM: It's the gun, it makes me feel so—FRIGHTENED!

BOYS: We see them all—we must take off, escape. These Go—Rillas, they take the strangest shape.

K-GAR OLLIE: I see them everywhere—they're stalking boys. These soldiers who would take our lives away. We must move fast, escape this war and then. We've got to get to Camp Kakuma. What's there? I fear I hope I hope I fear that there's the answer to our needs, but what'll we do if there's danger there and awful jungle noise? O, cattle dearest, we're so far away. We miss you, miss you. We just want to play.

The CHORUS OF CATTLE *appears.*

CHORUS: And so the boys trudged and crawled and marched and ran across the bush, dodging bullets, foraging for roots and the sometime berry, aiming their way to . . .

BOYS: Kakuma we thought was just a bit away. Not the thousand miles 'twas, the cattle didn't know.

CHORUS: And even if they could have gone as straight as a Masai spear. The armies, krypto armies, pseudo armies, would have stopped them in their tracks.

KRYPTO ARMY MEMBER: Stop!

A. I. JOSH: Not again.

KRYPTO ARMY MEMBER: Now you're ours, we need you for the fight.

CHORUS (to audience): And so they were conscripted by every remnant of every colonial power.

K-GAR OLLIE: What is "colonial"?

CHORUS: "Colonial" is when someone who is not from where you are comes to where you are and tells you what to do and say and think.

T-MAC SAM: I do not like that.

CHORUS: "Colonial" is someone coming to where you are and taking what is yours and telling you you better like it.

A. I. JOSH: That is something I do not like.

CHORUS: "Colonial" is someone coming to where you are and forcing you to work for them and taking all the things you make.

BOYS: That is all the things we do not like!

CHORUS: But for this moment, this precious fleeting moment, you have this moment to breathe before the next invasion takes you away.

A. I. JOSH: So let us form a camp so we may better protect ourselves.

T-MAC SAM: Let us cook a meal so that we may better fill our hungry selves.

"Lentils Onions Rice" rouses K-GAR OLLIE, *and he takes the lead on this song.*

K-GAR OLLIE: *If only we had lentils, onions, rice*
We'd have a lovely meal, o so nice
We'd put them in a pot and boil them, boil them hot
If we had a pot

If only we had lentils, onions, rice
If only we had spices and an herb
These roots, these flowers, weeds would taste
     Soup-Perb
If only we had lentils, onions, rice
How sweet to be our tongues,
when tasting something
O so nice
If only we had lentils, onions, rice
AND A POT!

A CRAZED BOY RADIO OPERATOR, *a young boy in a green smock and green plastic slippers—as someone wrote—looking like a deranged hospital orderly—stumbles on, a large battery atop his head.*

CRAZED BOY RADIO OPERATOR: I am the Radio Operator's Assistant. Have you seen him?

A. I. JOSH: Radio oper—what?

CRAZED BOY RADIO OPERATOR: All you need to do is plug me in. I have to get the message back.

He puts down the battery, sits, and ceremoniously empties his shoe of blood.

T-MAC SAM: You have put this thing upon the ground—

K-GAR OLLIE: And your hand is full of blood.

The CRAZED BOY RADIO OPERATOR *puts the shoe back on, the battery back on his head, and exits.*

CRAZED BOY RADIO OPERATOR *(exiting)*: I have to get the message back. I am the Radio Operator's Assistant. Have you seen him? Just plug me in.

The CRAZED BOY RADIO OPERATOR *exits.*

BOYS: And suddenly we had to leave this makeshift camp. Boys
    by the tens, hundreds pouring out of this makeshift camp. War
    in Ethiopia like Sudan before it. Soldiers driving us into Kenya
    south. Pushed to cross the Gilo River. The whole column of boys.
    Crocodiles snapping the surface beneath. Barely above the water
    was a bridge of swaying rope. We dozens hundreds clinging to
    each other without hope. Our tongues twisting in and out our
    lips blood across our teeth.

CHORUS: The crocodile has a toothsome smile
                He opens his mouth for all to see
                He shuts his mouth with you inside
                Your arm, your leg goes for a ride
                And all that's left for you to be
                Are stumps, your trunk and a little pile

A. I. JOSH: One boy grabbed my foot he would not let go
                On the bridge swaying splashing all my brains were
                    in my foot
                I shook I shook him off he grabbed again
                I hobbled forward dragging him along
                My foot my foot I had to have my foot
                Let go! I NEED MY FOOT!
                and then he was gone and I could move
                My chest hurt I couldn't catch my breath
                My foot felt for him I couldn't look my foot looked
                My foot couldn't find him
                I didn't even hear him cry
                Now I hear him cry
                Now I hear him cry
                He, my colleague, tells me he has drowned

SCENE: Camp Kakuma the City of Children

COPERNICUS PTOLEMY PATRICK *enters.*

COPERNICUS: Boys—hundreds thousands exhausted out of their skulls came to Camp Kakuma. They tripped slipped upon the dust the mud and fell to the ground some wearing little cloths around their middles and nothing more. One boy with a jaunty hat came with nothing else and did not seem to mind nor did the others. Another I recall kept flailing and rolling on the sand and pebbles and kept jolting up as if he'd had this hideous nightmare and kept screaming at the other boys to keep on singing, even though no one was singing. They lose their culture when they are driven so hard. They are mad and dangerous to themselves and you hope you hope they will pass out so that you can move them a bit and stroke their foreheads with a damp cloth. Then when they finally do, they either sleep fitfully so still like a stone so much that they appear dead. And some of them are. When the others awake, we give them broth, a little meat, gristle really, to try to build their strength. They are surprisingly strong, or at least resilient and in a few days they, some of them, even get a bit cheery. Others remain delirious. The boy who insisted upon the singing now just stares ahead. I am not hopeful he will come around.

Today is the first day of class. Yes, there is an attempt at schooling. I am Copernicus Ptolemy Patrick, headmaster. Good morning, class. You may say "Good Morning" back.

BOYS: Good morning back.

Good morning back.

COPERNICUS: I see. Just three of you today. Well, we have to begin somewhere. What are your names?

A. I. JOSH: A. I. Josh.

COPERNICUS: What does the A. I. stand for?

A. I. JOSH: What does the A. I. stand for. Stand for.

COPERNICUS: I see. And you?

T-MAC SAM: T. Mac Sam.

COPERNICUS: The "T" stands for—

T-MAC SAM: T.

COPERNICUS: And the Mac stands for—Mac. Alright, Sam. You, young man?

K-GAR OLLIE: K-Gar, stands for Kevin Garnett.

COPERNICUS: Who's he?

K-GAR OLLIE: I don't know.

COPERNICUS: What about numbers, that is, counting?

A. I. JOSH: One, two—eight!

COPERNICUS: OK, that needs some adjusting. The alphabet?

T-MAC SAM: Soup.

COPERNICUS: K-Gar?

K-GAR OLLIE (*singing*): Next time won't you sing with me?

COPERNICUS: How is it that you know these snippets? Where do you pick these things up? And how will we ever fill in the gaps? (*Speaks to the audience.*) The Boys worked very hard, and although their progress was slow, it was steady and in no time, well, years, really, they began to sound—rather like me.

A. I. JOSH: Mr. Copernicus Ptolemy Patrick, explain your name Copernicus to us. What, pray tell, does it stand for?

COPERNICUS: You explain it to me.

A. I. JOSH: He was a man who reversed the Ptolemaic system. Now explain to us who Ptolemy was?

COPERNICUS: Alright, I shall, seeing as how I think you're all bluffing—he was a man of ancient times.

T-MAC SAM: He devised a system of the universe that had the earth at

its center, with man at the center of the earth.

BOYS: Brilliant, my dear man, you have an excellent future ahead of you rotting right here at Camp Kakuma.

COPERNICUS (*to the audience*): The boys had a point, a painful one. The longer that they stayed at Kakuma, the more they learned— up to a point. In fact, they stopped learning because they ceased to see the point. When one war was supposedly over—

A BOY *rushes on.*

A BOY: The war is over! It's time to call it a day! DAY! Let's all return to our hearth and home 'cept no home and hearth exists. Let's stay right here at Kakuma Camp.

COPERNICUS: There's been a new development.

K-GAR OLLIE: What's a "development"?

COPERNICUS: It has to do with settlement.

T-MAC SAM: And what the hey is settlement?

COPERNICUS: It's when you're moved to safer places.

A. I. JOSH: Moved where?

COPERNICUS: To America.

T-MAC SAM: To A-m-e-r-i-c-a?

COPERNICUS: Chicago, Arlington, Massachusetts—

K-GAR OLLIE: That's where I want to go—Massa—Choo choo where the trains are—

A. I. JOSH: Chicago where the bulls are. I have read about this, where there are a lot of bulls.

COPERNICUS: Minny—Soda—where the tiny soft drinks are.

K-GAR OLLIE: Minny—Soda, what is that?

COPERNICUS: Where very light bright people with down upon their faces speak in strange high-pitched sing-song tongues.

K-GAR OLLIE: I do not want to go there. I have my own high pitch, and I am from the South where I want to stay.

COPERNICUS: And Fargo.

T-MAC SAM: Far Go? Go Far? How far far go?

COPERNICUS: Very farther than Ethiopia. No—Fargo is name of place.

K-GAR OLLIE: And how to get there? Why would we go to all these places? And who wants to take us there?

COPERNICUS: The Lutherans, the Catholics. They have a mission to save you—or at least give you the chance you don't have.

COPERNICUS *recedes, and the three* BOYS *are left alone. Our three* BOYS *sing a trio, a little of African Mills Brothers.*

BOYS: *Who are these Catho-licks and Luther Anns*
And what have they in mind for us, we fear
They have some plans, these Luther Anns they say
To work for them and herd their cows with sticks, blacks, tans
And what of Catho-licks who now abound
What if they want to take our souls and run
Why can't we have some fun
Just sitting in the sun
We're children, wanting all the wholes, the parts
You Catho-licks, you Luther Anns, your names
You drive us crazy, crazy with your games

COPERNICUS: They're not games. All of us—me here in Kakuma
in this makeshift room I call a "school." The well-meaning
missionaries so far from here. We don't pretend to think we're
saving lives. We only do a bit. We try to do our bit. Our little bit.
This tiny itsy bitsy spider bit. We're climbing up a waterspout,
and the drain is pouring out, and we the itsy bitsy spider climb
up the spout again.

SCENE: The Elders of the Tribe Just Say No

MIRIAM MAKER: We're sending you off but we won't lose you
We'll follow your progress and if you choose, you
Can be our leaders of the southern Sudanese
We're sorely short of leaders, tyrants have them
    on their knees
We're asking you politely when really what we
    mean
Is you have an obligation to save another teen
So go away and get your education proper
But we know that when you can return you must
Our many men who work the manganese and
    copper
Deserve your generosity, you now have all their
    trust

Some warnings few when in the USA
You'll be few boys inside of thousands mens
And ladies looking straight ahead
Big, tall—they cannot be, they seem
Glass buildings, bright lights, like you never
      fantasize
Don't go and be attracted by all play
Whatever they tell you, it's lies
Don't drink the beer, it's new to you
You'll burp like not before
There's something called "Fast Food and Drink"
      you'll slurp while craving more
And sweet things "Skittles" that they call
What they are, after all, I cannot tell at all
Just keep your wits about you when you dream
The thing you want the most is never what it
      seem

A bearded bony man—the JUSTICE MINISTER*—bursts upon the scene.*

JUSTICE MINISTER: Don't go at all, black boys
      There are many Negroes in those States
      Don't think you know them because of their hair
      They're not like us
      They sprinkle smelly things upon themselves
      They put these smelly things underneath their
        arms
      And then they rub them there and in their
        crotch
      They rub their behinds' cracks with white things
        made from trees
      Then they throw these white things down white
        holes
      And water rushes them away
      They are barbarians who have pulled up their
        African roots

And left them to rot in the sun

They would spoil the earth

They are not from here, they are not from there

MIRIAM MAKER: Who are you that you know so much?

JUSTICE MINISTER: Who are you?

MIRIAM MAKER: I am Miriam Maker, formerly of the Southern Sudanese Parliament, sent here to administrate this camp.

JUSTICE MINISTER: I AM THE Justice Minister from Khartoum, and I know that the Southern Sudanese Parliament no longer exists.

MIRIAM MAKER: You're telling me. And do you know, Bony Bearded Man, o you, the Justice Minister of Khartoum, the terrible injustice in and of these camps?

JUSTICE MINISTER: I know what I need to know. And there boys must not go.

MIRIAM MAKER: They are too precious to be left in harm's way.

JUSTICE MINISTER: And what of the others? Are they not precious too? Thousands, tens of thousands, how many can you save, if save is what you're doing?

MIRIAM MAKER: Among these boys is the future President of Southern Sudan.

JUSTICE MINISTER: There will be no Southern Sudan. It will all be destroyed by this war between those that smell one way, and those who smell the other.

MIRIAM MAKER: These boys are too precious to be left behind. That's just the way it is. Few are chosen and many are left behind.

JUSTICE MINISTER: And will these few return?

MIRIAM MAKER: I do not know. I DO know that THERE is a law and that here there is no law.

JUSTICE MINISTER: And if they do, will they be corrupt? Will they be common thieves?

MIRIAM MAKER: I do not know. I DO know that they are going to a land where they cannot just come and kill you.

JUSTICE MINISTER: And what of women who will tempt them so, with their tempting ways and their tempting dress?

MIRIAM MAKER: What are you speaking of? They have seen all the tempting dress and undress in the world. The women in the bush—what do they wear? Next to nothing.

JUSTICE MINISTER: You have been in the world?

MIRIAM MAKER: I have been in the world, and I have imagined all the rest.

JUSTICE MINISTER: They will come back, if they do, and they will bring revolution.

MIRIAM MAKER: True revolution. That is what I hope. These boys are off to a better life so that they might return and help us all to a better life.

JUSTICE MINISTER: Isn't it pretty to think so?

MIRIAM MAKER: Tomorrow when you are on the plane and
    traveling to the West
You'll then have been much farther—think that
    it's a test
Than any of your forbears ever dreamed that
    they would be
You'll be crossing oceans vast, 'though you've
    never seen the sea
A year will pass like nothing—at its end
You'll ask why we did not you, you, and you
    sooner send

SCENE: The March to the Plane of Josh, Sam, and Ollie

A. I. JOSH: The airplane's here. Let's march.

T-MAC SAM: It will come back. It will keep coming back.

K-GAR OLLIE: I'm not marching anywhere.

A. I. JOSH: It's not going to keep coming back, are you crazy? It's here once and then it's gone.

T-MAC SAM: It will come back. It will keep coming back.

K-GAR OLLIE: I've marched my whole life, and then some.

A. I. JOSH: And then some what? Don't you want to go to America? Don't you remember what Miriam Maker said?

A. I. AND K-GAR: "America is not a country where they can just come and kill you. They can't just come and kill you!"

T-MAC SAM: It will come back. I'll take the next one.

A. I. JOSH: It will not keep coming back. This is the first, last, and next one.

K-GAR OLLIE: How can it take all of us? There are hundreds, hundreds.

A. I. JOSH: That's why we have to march now. Miriam Maker said there is a law and here there is no law.

T-MAC SAM: A—m—e—r—i—c—a. I wrote it in the mud, on the wall.

K-GAR OLLIE: In America there are doors. I don't want doors.

A. I. JOSH: What do you mean "doors"? How do you know there are doors? What are doors to you and me?

T-MAC SAM: I'll take the next one. It will keep coming back.

A. I. JOSH: You are out of your skulls. It's time to move. March, walk, crawl, I don't care. The plane is taking us to . . .

A. I. AND T-MAC: A-m-e-r-i-c-a!

K-GAR OLLIE: In America there are doors. I don't want doors.

A. I. JOSH: You two, you two, you two repeat yourselves.

T-MAC AND K-GAR: You too, you too, you too repeat yourself.

A. I. JOSH: I've dreamt of this day for two whole years. Ever since I was—

T-MAC SAM: Ever since you were what?

A. I. JOSH: Twelve years old.

K-GAR OLLIE: I'm two years older than you, and I am staying put.

A. I. JOSH: Two years? What do you mean? I'm sixteen. I thought you were sixteen.

K-GAR OLLIE: I am. You're fourteen.

T-MAC SAM: I'm twelve. I haven't been dreaming of this moment for two whole years.

A. I. JOSH: I'm sixteen. That makes you twenty.

K-GAR OLLIE: Who says you're sixteen? You're fourteen and I'm sixteen, not twenty.

A. I. JOSH: I'm sixteen, not fourteen as you say I am, and you too, you too, you too are sixteen.

T-MAC SAM: I'm twelve.

A. I. JOSH: The airplane's here. The oldest goes first.

K-GAR OLLIE: Now I have you. If the oldest goes first, and you and I are the same age of sixteen, and Sam at twelve, then there IS no oldest, only the youngest Sam at twelve, so no one goes first, we don't march to the plane or march anywhere especially A-m-e-r-i-c-a, which can stay in the mud on the wall and never have doors. So there.

A. I. JOSH: Alright, you're twenty, I'm sixteen, Sam is twelve, you go first. Sam second, and I'm last.

T-MAC SAM: That would work nicely, if the plane weren't coming back, which of course it is, so it won't work nicely.

A. I. JOSH: It will work nicely, oldest, next oldest, next next oldest oldest.

The sound of an airplane engine.

T-MAC SAM: I wrote it in the mud, on the wall, A—m—e—r—i—c—a.

A. I. AND K-GAR: They can't just come and kill you.

A. I. JOSH: The airplane's really here. Let's march.

K-GAR OLLIE: Does the plane have a door? I don't want to sleep alone inside some plane behind a door.

A. I. JOSH: If there's a door, I'll open it. If there isn't, I'll open it anyway. Oldest first—Sam, Ollie, Josh, Josh, Sam, Ollie, Ollie, Josh, Sam, Josh—let's count—one three two, two three one—I'm frightened—

A ladder drops from the plane door.

A. I. JOSH: Just like the Gilo River. The Sudanese Liberation Army is chasing us, pushing us hard. We come to a rope ladder to climb up to the bridge, crocodiles below . . .

T-MAC SAM: This is a plane, this is not the Gilo, no crocodiles, no army chasing us, your foot won't be looking for your colleague.

K-GAR OLLIE: Not my foot—your foot and yours—I'm the oldest and I go first.

A. I. JOSH: You've changed your mind—hooray!

K-GAR OLLIE: Never any doubt—I'm going too!

T-MAC SAM: O, what the hey—

A. I. AND K-GAR: Hey Hey!

ACT TWO

SCENE: Dream Sequence. *The Wedding Dance in Camp Kakuma. A Chorus of high-jumping men—very Bill T. Jones—hopping, singing, chanting, clapping, shouting, leaping, weeping, howling, ululating. A. I. JOSH, in African garb.*

Nota bene: Nyandier rhymes with "Buy-land-see-air."

A. I. JOSH: I want to marry fair Nyandier.

NYANDIER, *an African Princess, appears.*

A. I. JOSH:　　　　Resplendent in her scent, the air is sweet
　　　　　　　　With sweat of dancing men who clap and leap
　　　　　　　　Who chant and sing and hop and ululate
　　　　　　　　Nyandier in splendid yellow dress, her hair
　　　　　　　　Done up, a gold stud dots her nose
　　　　　　　　Her toes, her ankles ringed, it makes me weep
　　　　　　　　Sweet Nyandier, I plant my flag in front of your
　　　　　　　　　　tent now
　　　　　　　　But here's your father old and he wants my only
　　　　　　　　　　cow
　　　　　　　　I'll twist and wave and shout and chant and sing
　　　　　　　　　　and howl and ululate
　　　　　　　　I'll leap and weep and gnash my teeth
　　　　　　　　And I'd give you my only cow
　　　　　　　　But I've nothing left to give
　　　　　　　　Won't you have me anyway and please forgive
　　　　　　　　　　cow's no longer now
　　　　　　　　My cow's no longer now.

T-MAC SAM *and* K-GAR OLLIE *wake* A. I. JOSH *from his dream. They're on the plane somewhere over the ocean. Ad-libbing, and then* . . .

T-MAC AND K-GAR: Josh Josh!

K-GAR OLLIE: It's OK, it's OK.

A. I. JOSH: I dreamt we were in Kakuma Camp.

T-MAC SAM: You need some sleep. Tomorrow. First day. This plane lands.

T-MAC AND K-GAR: We land.

BOYS: We land!

A. I. JOSH: I won't sleep.

K-GAR OLLIE: I will.

T-MAC SAM: I will.

T-MAC SAM *and* K-GAR OLLIE *sleep.* A. I. JOSH *sits up and, in best cow fashion, ruminates, as the plane's engines hum about them. Twenty-three hours later, in Fargo, North Dakota, the plane lands. COLD.*

A. I. JOSH: Would someone tell me please?
Is it day or is it night?
Are those shadows are those lights
How can anything be right
We have landed
We have landed
And now we're in the State Dakota North
Will we fight like in Sudan, South and North and
up and down
Will we war with South Dakota in the country
and in the town?
Are the many Christians in Pierre the ones we
now must hate
Are the Muslims North Dakotans there
The ones who share our fate?
Far Go, Go Far, North Dakot—to war!
Far Go Go Far, South Dakot—what for

Ahead of us is what we know at all—NOT!
And do we know exactly what we're in for—
is the South so very hot
What is this that makes this visit more than
    temporary, please
Explain it all to us poor boys
then explain it all AGAIN
Does nothing change from night to day
and all remain the same
Will we live inside this darkness still
and who is there to blame?

They're off the plane and met by CRISPUS ATTUCKS.

CRISPUS ATTUCKS: Crispus Attucks welcomes you to Fargo
    Coats warm coats for all when the winds do blow
        and they do blow across the plains up north
    Let's climb into my van and sally forth
    Please hurry, put on your coats and let's ride

The BOYS *are scrambling to put on coats.*

A. I. JOSH: Who's Sally Forth?

T-MAC SAM: His American girlfriend, remember we've been
warned.

K-GAR OLLIE: That's my red coat, the one with the bull.

A. I. JOSH: Here's the one I want.

T-MAC SAM: I'm sitting in the back, not next to Sally.

They all manage to scramble in CRISPUS'*s dilapidated van, with* T-MAC
shoved to the back.

CRISPUS ATTUCKS: This is a pretty nice town, I think you'll find.
    The wind blows, the trains rumble—make a
        heckuva sound—

You learn to like, not to mind.
The folks of Fargo smile, never frown—almost
Our diners are the friendliest around,
Excusin' the occasional burnt toast
Ten minutes and we're there
Need anything, just blare

A. I. JOSH (*inside his head*): Who is this—what is this—why am I
here?

T-MAC SAM (*inside his head*): Why am I here—what is this—who is
this?

K-GAR OLLIE (*inside his head*): What is this—who is this—why am I
here?

A. I. JOSH (*inside his head*): My heart's so cold, my black lips purple/
blue.

T-MAC SAM (*inside his head*): My neck is so cold, my knees, only my
tongue is warm.

K-GAR OLLIE (*inside his head*): What is cold—why am I cold—why
does cold live here?

A. I. JOSH (*inside his head*): I was so eager to rush on that plane.

T-MAC SAM (*inside his head*): I must concentrate on my tongue.

K-GAR OLLIE (*inside his head*): I must think about this cold.

A. I. JOSH (*inside his head*): Kakuma Camp so far away.

T-MAC SAM (*inside his head*): Kakuma Camp so far away.

K-GAR OLLIE (*inside his head*): Kakuma Camp so far away.

A. I. JOSH (*inside his head*): What's he saying? Does everyone talk
this way?

T-MAC SAM (*inside his head*): What's he saying? Does everyone talk
this way?

K-GAR OLLIE (*inside his head*): What's he saying?

A. I. JOSH (*inside his head*): Is he one of those Negroes with the hair
like ours we were warned against?

T-MAC SAM (*inside his head*): Is he one of those Negroes with the lips
like ours we've been warned against?

K-GAR OLLIE (*inside his head*): Is he one of those Negroes when you
scrape the skin you find he's white?

A. I. JOSH *(inside his head)*: Why can't Copernicus be with us now, making sense, making peace?

T-MAC SAM *(inside his head)*: Why can't Copernicus be with us now, making sense, making peace?

BOYS: Why can't Copernicus be with us now, making sense, making peace? Do we maybe see some light over there. Are our eyes so now accustomed to the dark. Will we ever think of something before this land. Like our elders their cataracts cloud their eyes. Will we ever see an animal who sparkles in the sun. Will we ever put our heads to the sides of cattle lowing, and rest such rest we lose all sense of hurt. Even flies that buzz about and gather 'round the eyes of our favorite bulls would be so welcome now, we'd never more complain, we wouldn't even shoo them gone. They are life, part of all we are. What are we part of now. Do we have a part that's ours. Have we ever had a part that's ours. What are we part of now.

CRISPUS ATTUCKS: I'm pullin' us in
So put on a grin
Home Sweet Home is where you at
What crosses our path but a big black cat!

The van screeches to a halt.

SCENE: Aren't You Glad We Came This Far?

CLAYTON POWELL, *from Social Reach.*

CLAYTON: I'm Clayton Powell, your most obedient servant from Social Reach. It's my job to set you up since you landed on our concrete beach. This is your apartment for the next six weeks.

BOYS: Apartment?

CLAYTON: It has running water hot and cold, and its faucet never leaks.

BOYS: Running water.

CLAYTON: Here's a bedroom with a door you close to keep the world outside.

BOYS: Door!

CLAYTON: Here's a bathroom with a door you close to maintain all your pride.

BOYS: Door!

CLAYTON: Here's the kitchen with a microwave with a pretty door, refrigerator with doors of two.

BOYS: Door!

CLAYTON: Open it up inside and here's another door for you.

BOYS: Door!

CLAYTON: A table chairs and silverware though plastic forks you'll have to make them do. The cabinets with doors hold food you've never seen.

BOYS: Doors!

CLAYTON: Beans in cans, soup in packs, ketchup in a widemouth jar.

BOYS: Widemouth jar.

CLAYTON: Mayonnaise and mustard / sour cream potatoes into chips.

BOYS: Chips.

CLAYTON: Cheerios granola bars and salsa spicy dips.

BOYS: Dips.

CLAYTON: Aren't you glad you came this far? No turning back just turning front. No turning back this is the hunt.

BOYS: Hunt!

CLAYTON: The clock is set, the radio on, the snooze alarm will wake you from your slumber. Are there any questions now?

BOYS: Yeah yeah (Ad-lib questions.)

CLAYTON: It's really / awfully simple / quite straightforward / awfully simple / quite a piece of cake. O here's the thermostat in case you want more heat.

BOYS: Heat, heat.

CLAYTON: If there's anything you want to hear again I'm so glad to repeat.

BOYS: Yeah, yeah

CLAYTON: It's all within my mission here, all so true to form. I think you'll find this country great, A. I., T-Mac, and Kaygar.

A. I. JOSH: A. I.

T-MAC SAM: T-Mac

K-GAR OLLIE: Kevin Garnett

CLAYTON: I'll check on you tomorrow morn
           You'll be glad for the day you were born
           This is the first night of the rest of your lives
           This ain't the last night so don't break out
                in hives
           Aren't you glad you came this far?

BOYS: Aren't we glad we came this far?

SCENE: A. I. JOSH, T-MAC SAM *huddle together on the couch.* K-GAR OLLIE *is feeling around the small apartment, its walls, its floors, its ceilings.*

K-GAR OLLIE: Therm—o—stat—what is that? In case we want more heat. He so glad to repeat. We want heat—floor is cold—Up turn heat—Just doing what we're TOLD!

K-GAR OLLIE *gleefully cranks up the heat and dives onto the couch, where all three huddle together. The morning after. The* BOYS *are asleep. Doorbell. No response from the* BOYS. *Again the doorbell. Again, no response. Pounding on door. Key in lock.*
    Enter CLAYTON POWELL.

CLAYTON: Hey, guys! It's scorching, open the windows! (*Looking at the thermostat.*) It's ninety-five! Are you out of your skulls? (*Opening the windows.*) Aren't you just boiling?

K-GAR OLLIE: Boiling, scorching, out of our skulls, when do we eat?

T-MAC SAM: Finally warm and you let in the cold, when do we eat?

A. I. JOSH: Ninety-five, what is that, when do we eat?

CLAYTON: Eat, when did you eat—

BOYS: When—DO—we—eat!

A. I. JOSH: I must ask you something, Mr. Clayton Powell—

CLAYTON: You already have—I know—When do you EAT? And why haven't you yet?

A. I. JOSH: Are you here to bring us our food?

BOYS: Where is it?

CLAYTON:
Your food is here
And it's clear
You haven't eaten anything, you sat here
huddled all the night
milk undrunk and out of sight.

BOYS: Our food is where?

CLAYTON *starts pulling cans from the shelves.*

BOYS: We do not see it!

From left to right, K-Gar Ollie (Samuel G. Roberson Jr.), A. I. Josh (André Samples), and T-Mac Sam (Namir Smallwood) discover, for the first time, modern conveniences like refrigerators and Cheez-Its in their Fargo apartment. Photograph by Rob Levine.

CLAYTON: You boys have escaped lions—

BOYS: Lions fierce—

CLAYTON: Marauding guerrillas—

BOYS: Machine-gun–happy doped-up soldiers—

CLAYTON: Poisonous snakes—

BOYS: Deadly adders—

CLAYTON: And you're telling me you do not know how to open a can?

BOYS: Yes! Yes!! YES!!!

CLAYTON:
>Well, knock me over with a wet noodle
>I do apologize for the kit and caboodle
>Not much of a guide to your new land
>Welcome to the world of keys and locks
>Let's practice openin' this big bad box
>Gather 'round, boys and boys
>this here's your introduction
>to the great American production
>Instant food with attitude!

BOYS: Instant food with attitude!

A. I. JOSH: Now may we close the window?

T-MAC SAM: And turn up the therm

K-GAR OLLIE: With food in our bellies, coats on our backs. There's nothing on earth that we will not lack?

CLAYTON POWELL *starts showing the* BOYS *"How."*

SCENE: The BOYS in Academia

MOIRA MIDNIGHT, *the Student Placement Officer, greets the* BOYS *at the school's entrance. They are quite the curiosity pieces, with students and teachers rubbernecking to see what they are "really" like.*

MOIRA: Gentlemen, you've promptly arrived—congrats. I'm Moira Midnight, Student Placement Officer. We can't tell you how thrilled we are to see you here at our fair school in our fair town.

Though we're at the far end of our fair town, it's fair to say that we're not too far from the center of things, the center being smack dab at the very beginning of that which holds and binds us all to each other and energizes us all in ways too numerous to enumerate fairly and fully at the present time so without farther, or further, ado I'll take you to your homerooms and . . .

MOLLY *enters.*

MOLLY: Mom! I forgot to tell you I need money for the . . . Oh! Sorry!
MOIRA: Molly! You're here now, so come on. Meet A. I. Josh, T-Mac and K-Gar. This is Molly Midnight. Who happens to be my daughter and a potential classmate of yours.

MOLLY *and the* BOYS *shake hands. Greetings. Timidity. Excitement.*

MOLLY: All your names are really cool. A. I. T-Mac. K-Gar—all basketball names.
BOYS: Basketball names?
MOLLY: Your folks must have been really cool.
A. I. JOSH *(eager to please)*: Yes! Our folks were cool!
K-GAR OLLIE: Very cool. Very cold. Dead!
MOLLY: Oh my gosh. Yes, I know. My mom told me a little about, well, what you've been through. Then I insert foot in mouth. You know that expression? The very first time we speak, I make a terrible impression. I'm pleased to meet you and excited you're here. You hear? Fargo is fine but kind of a bore. I just feel like I'm ready, you know? For something more. I want to spread my wings, 'til everyone sings.
MOIRA: Molly, stop, the first bell has rung and you all need to go. I'll take you boys to your homerooms. There'll be tests later to see where you place. I think you'll do nicely, you each have a nice face.
A. I. JOSH *(to himself as he follows after Moira)*: Molly Midnight. In a yellow dress. With jewelry, gold and silver, and her hair. Just like in my dream of Nyandier.

A boy approaches and stops them in their tracks.

RUMMY: Name's Rummy, rhymes with Dummy, but ironically, if you
    know what that means, I'm not one. Quite the smartest bloke
    about, rest assured. So, what're the capitals of Mozambique,
    Chad, Zambia, Botswana, and Burkina Faso, the poorest nation
    per capita on earth?

BOYS: Maputo, N'Djamena, Lusaka, Gaborone, Ouagadougou.

RUMMY: I think you'll do, as Moira Midnight would have it, you'll do
    quite nicely-nicely. Hey, let me show you how Fargo plays.
    Tonight I'll take you to the Kaos and Kakofoney Kafay.

*They all move to the classroom, where they take seats among their perhaps
about-to-be fellow students and try not to look about too much. The cries
and whispers, or at least the whispers, begin.*

SCENE: The K(aos) & K(akofoney) Kafay.

RUMMY *escorts the Boys into the K & K Kafay. Whence Postal Modern
Bedlam and Pandemonium reign. Twelve-year-old white kids seated at
komputer war games shouting, kicking, whirling around in their swivel
chairs, banging the chairs against walls, wailing in delight, squealing in
pain, but NEVER getting out of their chairs. The* BOYS *can only stare.*

RUMMY: Take a machine!

RUMMY *pushes the boys in front of three machines, whirls them around
in their chairs three times, and then "lands" them in front of the screens.*
RUMMY *is the only one standing, orchestrating, controlling. A flurry of
lines pour forth from the machines.*

MACHINE: The goddess breathes and evermore
                      Your building is complete
                      Our warriors have engaged the enemy
                      Ah, the great outdoors

> Your building is complete
> Our sacred land is being desecrated

A huge burst of gunfire. Intensified hollering, hooting hooligan howling from the white kids, subsiding but only a bit. Again, the machine voices as the games kick it back.

MACHINE: We must act Onward!
             We are pleased to strike
             I am vigilant
             Research finished
             Your building is complete
             Our sacred land is being desecrated
             Your building is complete

A. I. JOSH, T-MAC SAM, *and* K-GAR OLLIE *are getting into the games. Again the machine voices.*

MACHINE: We are poised to strike
             I stand ready
             Ah, the great outdoors
             Our warriors have engaged the enemy
             Your building is complete
             The goddess breathes and evermore
             We are poised to strike
             Your building is complete
             I stand ready
             Research finished
             Our sacred land is being desecrated
             The goddess breathes and evermore
             Your building is complete
             Ah, the great outdoors

A huger burst of gunfire. The screws turned tighter than tight as adolescent war cries punch the air. Again, none of the boys leaves his seat. Every ounce of energy is concentrated sedentarily. Only RUMMY *stands and twirls the boys about, left to right and right to left.* K-GAR OLLIE *tries to stand.* RUMMY *pushes him back down. Then* A. I. JOSH—*the same thing. Then* T-MAC SAM—*the same.* A. I. JOSH, T-MAC SAM, *and* K-GAR OLLIE *all stand together.* RUMMY *can't push them all back down.* K-GAR OLLIE *bursts for the door, as if to throw up. The gunfire increases.*

 T-MAC SAM *and* A. I. JOSH *race after him, sending* RUMMY *slamming to the floor.* RUMMY *rights himself, now furious, and we see the real boy gesturing obscenely after the boy and shouting racial epithets, now drowned in the War Games of the machines as one last word comes from the machine.*

MACHINE: Ah, the great outdoors

The white kids let out one last burst of puerile excitement.

K-GAR OLLIE: This is America? Games in which you pretend to kill these darting, little screaming creatures. This is the land of madness our Elders warned us against!

SCENE: Extracurriculars

BOYS: We're all in school in different ways, though often in the same classrooms. We walk the halls, eyes to the floor. Then twirl the combination rusty locker locks. Those locks, those locks, confusing. We go to gym.
K-GAR OLLIE: There are lots of doors. And the games, are winning or losing. That girl . . .
T-MAC SAM: . . . that other girl . . .

K-GAR OLLIE: Some, our so-called classmates, one who mocks
        Me and the way I speak, says that he'll box
        Me, kicking speech right off my tongue and yet
        When I look at him twice—"You've lost the bet"
        Says three or four other boys as he skulks
        Away—they look at me and shrug—these hulks.

BOYS: When our classes, finally, are done. We find out there is more. After school Ak—Ti—Vi—Tees? Called Extra—Core—Ika—Lore???

T-MAC SAM: I choose a sport—basketball. The coach smiled when he passed me in the hall.

A. I. JOSH: For me, it's 4-H—health, head, hands, heart—I have all these things, so I have a good start.

K-GAR OLLIE: Miss Midnight said that with my kind face.
        Community service was my best place.

MOIRA MIDNIGHT *enters.*

MOIRA MIDNIGHT: You'll be serving meals at this homeless shelter, Holy Apostles Soup Kitchen. Not the fair far end, but the fair middle of town. Smack dab in the middle. Where outreach-in reach needs to reach.

K-GAR OLLIE *serving food at the Holy Apostles Soup Kitchen.*

K-GAR OLLIE: A scoop of mashed potatoes gravy green
        These gray little dots they're really peas
        Steam Table Ollie, set before these piles
        Who are these folks, what did that old man say?
        His color gray, like sick Ayoun, the lean
        He wanted meat, without the fat; the miles
        I've come, meals I've not seen in the bush
        Days went by, a few gourds and seeds—and who's
        This wretched man with these open sores
        My god my god, wheelchair, please don't push
        That poor person out of the way, his shoes
        On backwards—stop this, please open the doors
        I can't be in this place, I'll surely die
        You must, these doors, please push them open,
         let me fly.

A. I. JOSH *at his 4-H club meeting with a sad-looking American cow.*

A. I. JOSH: Ayoun, please help me now, they want me to care for this cow. She cannot yield. Her milk is dry. I could leave her be, let her die. I can't help her, look, she's wheezing; Ayoun, please. Tell me what to do!

AYOUN: A. I. Josh, I come to you from beyond
A. I., it's soon this cow will moo no more
But she has one thing left so don't ignore
Embrace this beast; give your all,
The prize in her eyes is what you'll lead her
to win
In memory of me, your Ayoun, don't give her up.

AYOUN *disappears.*

A. I. JOSH: Thank you, Ayoun! This cow is my kith and kin. This 4-H contest—I'll take her all the way. I am back with my cow and here I shall stay.

T-MAC SAM *in basketball practice. The* COACH *watches from the side.*

COACH: Bunny Shots Bunny Shots
Tie their jocks in knots
Take it to the Hole
Deliver that Rock
Kiss that glass
Pass pass pass
Arms up—Block
Backdoor screen
Point guard mean
Zone defense man to man

T-MAC SAM *(in the midst of it)*:
Take it to the Hole

Take it to the Hole
Sam for the Jam now take it to the Hole
Let that rock do its rotation
I'm The Basketball Man, the Best in the Nation
Since first creation, I am sensation
Cause I'm Sam the man
And I've come to my calling in life
I'm a B-Ball player Extraordinaire, the newest
    of Air
And I'm leaving behind, behind all strife

He throws the ball and, almost accidentally, he makes a basket. He does a chant or cheer or a dance. Very Sudanese. Then feels the others watching him. He stops. The ball hits him, thrown from offstage while he stands still. The COACH *blows the whistle.*

COACH: Sam, you forgot to switch
                      What you doin', standin' around, scratchin'
                          some itch?
                      YOU DO THIRTY LAPS
                      WIND SPRINTS AT THAT
                      You got to get down that BODY FAT
                      And be here tomorrow two hours early
                      for some Real Victorious Purlie
                      And you better damn well
                      Come in with some FEAR

T-MAC SAM *starts his wind sprints.*
    K-GAR OLLIE *in study hall, dressed completely in black. We hear what he's reading and then we're in his thoughts.*

K-GAR OLLIE: "Seems, Madam? Nay, it is. I know not 'seems.'
                      'Tis not alone my inky cloak, good mother,
                      Nor customary suits of solemn black.
                      Together with all forms, moods, shapes of grief

That can denote me truly. These indeed seem,
For they are actions that a man might play;
But I have that within that passeth show—
These but the trappings and the suits of woe."
I need no inky cloak, my birthday suit of solemn
    black
I have no actions that a man might play
I will not wheeze or roll upon my back
I'll find the words express my thoughts, I'll say,
Holy Apostle's Kitchen, show me how
To live with soup—I must, I think, do it
Is this a revelation and should I push right
    through it?

MOIRA MIDNIGHT *arrives.*

MOIRA: I want to know about your first day with soup, so to speak,
but I also want to know about these Elders who warned you boys
about this country's and people's evils. What did they say to you?

K-GAR OLLIE: They told us not to drink the beer, that it would make
us sick.

MOIRA: It's like rancid bubble water, so they're right on with that
advice. But I can't believe that that seemed their direst warning.

K-GAR OLLIE: "Seemed, Madam? Nay it was. I know not seemed."

MOIRA: Ah, very clever, K-Gar, perhaps you should be a writer.
Reading Shakespeare's HAMLET, are you?

K-GAR OLLIE: Yes.

MOIRA: Do you find it difficult?

K-GAR OLLIE: No. I like the way the words click and bounce. Rather
like our African tongues, wrapping my African lips around these
bouncings and clickings. "The Play's the Thing wherein I'll
Catch the Conscience of the King."

A bell rings.

MOIRA: Have to go—come to me later about Holy Apostles. "Good K-Gar, keep thy knighted color on and let thine eye look like a friend on Fargo."

K-GAR OLLIE: My skin of solemn black, my inky cloak
                 What do you make of me, you Fargo folk

MOIRA *exits.*

SCENE: MOLLY MIDNIGHT *and* A. I. JOSH *enter from opposite direction.*

MOLLY: Hi Hi, A. I.
A. I. JOSH: Hi Hi Moll-I, I mean Moll-ee
MOLLY: Did you get your Sosh done? Wasn't it really hard? And that second one?
A. I. JOSH: Sosh? So—see—o—lowgee? Oh—I didn't do it.
MOLLY: Want me to help you? I could help you if you want. Let's sit right down and do it.

She sits on the ground and motions him down and down he goes.

A. I. JOSH: I was doing something else. I have this for you.

He hands her a sort of necklace.

A. I. JOSH: It's just on a string. You could put it on something else.
MOLLY: But what is it?
A. I. JOSH: It's a heart that's been hardened. From a bird that we ate.
MOLLY: You ate the bird but hardened the heart and saved it? Why—how—did you do that? And won't it decay?
A. I. JOSH: But then I'd get you another. I'd kill it and eat it—
MOLLY: That's enough. I don't know that I'll want another, but thank you for this. I'll keep it.

MOLLY*'s not sure what to make of this.* A. I. JOSH *is proud of what he's done but a bit puzzled.*

T-MAC SAM: I'm in some clanging classroom—like you'd
              say—ZOO
              And all my past come flooding and pent-up
              feelings
              Make me ice cold
              And now I worry to pay the rent
              I don't get the "bought and sold"
              Some say, don't bother
              I say let the rock be rolled
              I'm in this country of the Big Tent
              Melting pot—well, break the mold
              U.S. one hundred thousand percent

SCENE: One Month Later the BOYS Cook In

T-MAC SAM *and* K-GAR OLLIE *and* RUMMY *sit in the glow of the TV.* A. I.
JOSH *enters with* MOLLY. *Both carry grocery bags.*

K-GAR OLLIE: These bills, these bills. How am I suppose to pay all
    these bills?

T-MAC SAM: Don't look at me. I don't have any more money—I sent it
    all to Kakuma Camp.

K-GAR OLLIE: Well, we need money.

T-MAC SAM: I need to eat—Where is Josh?

RUMMY: He's bringing dinner, right? Usually when you invite
    someone to your home at night, dinner is implied.

A. I. JOSH: Tonight we eat things not in tins. Tinny tinned food.

MOLLY: Canned food. Josh and I have some lentils and rice and
    onions.

A. I. JOSH: And?

MOLLY: Spices. Josh says he's making a traditional meal.

A. I. JOSH: Not out of tin—tinny, makes our stomachs sick. You,
    Sam, Ollie, and Rummy, you make everything.

He starts to go toward the bedroom.

MOLLY: I thought YOU were making it, with me assisting.

A. I. JOSH: Alright, I'll get it going. Sam, Ollie, move! And Rummy, dude, you start chopping.

T-MAC SAM *bursts out.*

T-MAC SAM: I want Kakuma back, back to Kakuma Camp. We don't get enough to eat here.

A. I. JOSH *is preparing the meal in all its details. This should be realistic—smelling the frying onions, et cetera.*

K-GAR OLLIE: These bills—these food stamps. They keep sticking to my pocket. I was better off when I had no pockets. And money for rent. I want to pay in cowrie shells. Keep these lights on—pay for electricity—what are they called—utilizers—we are being utilized!

T-MAC SAM: I go into the cafeteria and sit in front of a mound of mushed potatoes with brown water in the middle spilling over and everyone is chattering around me.

MOLLY: The first three months, they're the hardest.

RUMMY: Then the next fifteen years.

A. I. JOSH: Here, stir. I have to go prepare myself. Sam, Ollie, show her and Rummy the African dice game. And you master complainer chop chop.

A. I. JOSH *goes to the bedroom.*

T-MAC SAM: Oh, this is a good one. We'll teach you to play in no time.

T-MAC SAM *sets out the dice.*

MOLLY *(stirring)*: What's it called?

T-MAC SAM: Farkle.

K-GAR OLLIE: Farkle—in Fargo—we played it in Kakuma—we called it KooKooRooku in Kakuma.

T-MAC SAM: Just watch and we will teach you. Take these dice.

MOLLY: I can't really stir and play at the same time.

K-GAR OLLIE: We'll play for you. You just keep stirring.

K-GAR OLLIE throws the dice down.

K-GAR OLLIE: Farkle!

T-MAC SAM: Molly, you lost.

MOLLY: Already?

K-GAR OLLIE: Again.

He throws the dice down.

K-GAR OLLIE: Farkle!

T-MAC SAM: Molly, again.

MOLLY: Farkle!

T-MAC SAM: How you figure?

MOLLY: Well—ah—I thought if I said it—

T-MAC AND K-GAR: You didn't Farkle. You didn't even Kookoorooku.

A. I. JOSH comes out of the bedroom. He is in traditional African robe, a bright green with matching kufi.

K-GAR OLLIE: Josh, you put us all to shame. How did you get such beautiful threads? That is what we call them in America, Molly.

A. I. JOSH: You could have had the same. How do you like this brilliant color, Molly? Ollie, I traded my rations, as you well know, food rations, for this robe—worth it, every bite I did not take—and you know it—and wish it were yours.

The doorbell rings. Here is KOOKOOROOKU, the real gamester. A. I. JOSH opens the door to a young Sudanese man dressed in down-at-the-mouth hip-hop duds. The young man and the three Boys embrace.

A. I. JOSH: Molly, this is the REAL Kookoorooku, named after the game.

KOOKOOROOKU: The game's named after me, my brother. What you cookin' for Kookoo?

MOLLY: Hi, I'm Molly.

KOOKOOROOKU: Enchanté.

RUMMY: Rummy.

KOOKOOROOKU: Well named. Koo to you too. Nice to meet you and nice to be met. Let's eat.

The BOYS pile on food.

MOLLY: So, Koo, may I call you that?

KOOKOOROOKU: Call me. But don't call me Late for Dinner. Hey, Molly, you get it?

MOLLY: How long have you been here?

KOOKOOROOKU: About ninety seconds, but you were here before me, so you must have been here about two minutes.

MOLLY: Do you live by yourself?

KOOKOOROOKU: I do now. I didn't then, Girl friend. When I first came to town, I shacked up, you know, with The Family Knudsen.

A. I. JOSH: Sven!

T-MAC SAM: Karin!

ALL: And the Twins!

MOLLY: What were they like?

KOOKOOROOKU: They were NICE. So NICE it drove Kookoorooku cuckoo, truth be told.

A. I. JOSH: Cuckoo!

T-MAC SAM: Cuckoo for Kookoorooku!

A. I. JOSH: Tell Molly the killer hippo story.

KOOKOOROOKU: Ah, yes, the Killer Hippo Story! Well, We were having a traditional Fargo Feast, and it's actually quite tasty, and we're passing the Hamburger Helper and Mr. Knudsen—

A. I. JOSH: Sven.

KOOKOOROOKU: Sven! Says, *(He imitates the pompous Mr. K.)* "So, Koo, are you finding your classes for your GED challenging?"

And I said (*Very straightforward.*) "I am a bit bored, but I am working hard because I don't want to go back to the killer hippos." And Mrs. Knudsen says (*He imitates her overbearing sincerity.*) "Tell us all about the killer hippos, Koo." And so I told them how this not very large killer hippo, but not very terribly friendly, charged my friend and me. How I climbed up a tree and watched as, below me, this killer hippo tore my friend to pieces. Just chopped him in half.

And the Knudsens just sat there, and then Sven said, "Well, that's quite a tale, Koo." And Mrs. Knudsen said, "It's really wonderful what we can learn from you, Koo." And then one twin said, "Ooooh, I know all about hippos, too, Koo! I went with the Girl Scouts to the Fargo zoo!" and the other twin said, "Ooooooh, I know even more about hippos, Koo!

BOYS (*finishing the twin's line with Koo*): . . . I've seen *The Lion King* fifteen times!"

KOOKOOROOKU, A. I. JOSH, *and* T-MAC SAM *sing* The Circle of Life. A. I. JOSH *and* T-MAC SAM *engage in gesticulatory male bonding of a highly individualized nature with* KOOKOOROOKU. MOLLY *joins in.* K-GAR OLLIE *does not.*

KOOKOOROOKU: Ollie, Ollie, why do you not join in?

K-GAR OLLIE: Too easy, Koo. Too easy to make fun. And you, Molly, what do you find so funny? These Foster Family souls, they are your people, are they not? And what about you Rummy? Where do you come from?

RUMMY: Like my old man? He's alright when he's around, which he's not, so he isn't, and he won't be, so he won't be.

K-GAR OLLIE: So why laugh?

T-MAC SAM: Because it's funny.

K-GAR OLLIE: And it's serious.

T-MAC SAM: And it's funny AND it's serious. Yes, we all want to go back, and we all want to be here, so it's funny, and it's sad, and yes we have to be able to laugh.

K-GAR OLLIE: Yes, I want to laugh too. But not at the—what is the word, Molly, you should know?

MOLLY: Expense. You don't want to laugh at the expense of others.

K-GAR OLLIE: People who are trying to do the right thing.

A. I. JOSH: Look at what I wear. Seven days' rations to get my robe, my hat, THAT is doing the right thing. We are ALL doing the right thing—the Fosters and the Knudsens and the Midnights and the Kookoorookus, and We Lost Boys.

KOOKOOROOKU: We Lost Boys. B-O-Y-Z. We're in this country, and yes, Ollie, there are people trying to do the right thing, and yes, Molly, I've been here for a year, and I love to sing and dance and jive you 'til you're jived, joved, jiven. And all the while, it's not easy here, not easy—but it's free.

RUMMY: It's free and it's the home of the brave.

KOOKOOROOKU: Dig dugger duggest. Kookoorooku back achoo.

BOYS, MOLLY, AND RUMMY: Dig dugger duggest. We did Kookoorooku too.

A. I. JOSH: And one last, one Lost Thing. Where's all the food? Rummy!

And, indeed, they do.

SCENE: A. I. JOSH and MOLLY MIDNIGHT clean up after the party.

MOLLY *and* A. I. JOSH *washing dishes.* A. I. *still in his ceremonial robes.*

MOLLY: These robes, A. I. Is this what you would wear every day at home?

A. I. JOSH: No, Molly. For special occasions only. For gatherings or dances in my village.

MOLLY: We do that too, you know. Get dressed up for dances and celebrations. Has anyone at school told you about Prom?

A. I. JOSH: Prom? No, Molly. Please, you tell me.

MOLLY: It's a dance. To celebrate the end of school, I guess. I could show it to you. Would you like to go as my date?

A. I. JOSH: I would like that, yes.

MOLLY: OK then! You have your ceremonial garb already! I'll have to get mine. And then we can go. Together.

A. I. JOSH: It will be my first time at a dance like this.

MOLLY: I have a feeling it will feel like my first time too. We'll make it special. Different.

A. I. JOSH: I'd like that.

MOLLY: Me too.

She kisses him on the cheek.

SCENE: The End of the Season

A. I. JOSH, T-MAC SAM, *and* K-GAR OLLIE *pile into their apartment. It's homier, in an American way, than we remember.*

T-MAC SAM: Oh, what a season!

K-GAR OLLIE: This year is almost over.

T-MAC SAM: Sam the man, put it in the hole, nothing but net! Look out here it comes, I'm in the Summer League, Connecticut, play against the best.

K-GAR OLLIE: I'm going to Northern Michigan and studying Latvian.

A. I. JOSH: La—Latvian?

T-MAC SAM: Next fall I got a scholarship to Lower Southern Mississippi Polytechnical Evangelical Reformed Christian Academy Junior College in Division Three.

K-GAR OLLIE: I'm good at languages, and I'm learning Latvian so that I can someday deliver sermons in the Latvian Lutheran Church in Fargo, North Dakota, our hometown!

A. I. JOSH: Since when are you good at languages and are you sure that there is such a thing as what—and this is our what?

K-GAR OLLIE: Hometown.

A. I. JOSH: Home—town. This is a town, and this is where we live— our Livetown. Sam, when are you going and where?

T-MAC SAM: Coach told me today—I'll start as point guard, spend two years, and then move to Division One. Aren't you guys getting my lingo? I have a scholarship to—

K-GAR AND A. I.: Lower Southern Polytechnical Evangelical Reformed Christian Academy Junior College in Division Three in the Great State of MissiPPISSI—dass M-I-S-S-I-P-P-I-S-S-I!!!

T-MAC SAM: Don't make fun—DON'T MAKE FUN!!! Josh, what are you going to do next year? You're eighteen and counting and you can barely count!

A. I. JOSH: I'm going to the Wild West for the last Great Cattle Drive, and I'm going to be with the American relatives of Ayoun.

T-MAC SAM: You are out of your mind.

A. I. JOSH: And you aren't?

K-GAR OLLIE: There are no American relatives of Ayoun.

A. I. JOSH: There are tens of thousands, and I'm going to be with them all.

T-MAC SAM: This IS the Wild West! This is NORTHWEST WILD DAKOTA!!!

A. I. JOSH: This is tame. This is a town. I don't want town. I want range, movement, the way we used to move with all of our cattle and sleep in the open against their sides, lean on them, and they used to low, so softly, and there's nothing like that in this America.

T-MAC SAM: There's nothing like that—

K-GAR AND T-MAC: In this America—right here.

BOYS: Nothing like that!

T-MAC SAM (*to A. I. JOSH*): So does that mean you aren't going to the Prom?

K-GAR OLLIE: Someone's not going to the Prom?

A. I. JOSH: I don't know—

T-MAC SAM: What do you mean, you don't know? You've been saving and preening, when not seen, of course . . .

A. I. JOSH: How do you know?

K-GAR OLLIE: You mean about Molly Midnight, Moira's daughter? A little bird told us.

RUMMY *enters.*

K-GAR AND T-MAC: Hi, Little Bird!

Tableau. MOLLY MIDNIGHT *as* NYANDIER, *that is, in complete African wedding dress.* A. I. JOSH *in his African garb. He bows. She curtsies. They link arms and promenade to the Prom.*

MOLLY: So you think your love for cows isn't mad. It's not some disease that you shouldn't try to rid yourself of once and for all—Jeez!

A. I. JOSH: I'm not saying, Molly, it isn't bad, in a way, but it's good too, I can't lie. It's where I come from, it's who I am, please.

MOLLY: I'm trying to understand, but competing with a cow, is just not what I've wanted MOST.

A. I. AND MOLLY: I wish I'd never left the Sudan / I wish you'd never come to Fargo

A. I. JOSH: I wish I could go back.

MOLLY: I wish you'd just go back to your cow.

A. I. JOSH: There's no back to go to and how do you think I could ever go back?

MOLLY: What do you mean, there's always a back to go to—cow SCHMOW!

A. I. JOSH: There's no back, there's no front—don't you get it? There's no village, Ayoun is dead.

MOLLY: What a terrible thing—in my whole life, I never thought about this.

A. I. JOSH: It's just about all I think about—and you, I think about you.

MOLLY: Thank you. That's sweet. I think about you, too. A lot. Perhaps we shouldn't fight anymore.

A. I. JOSH: Perhaps—

MOLLY: What do you mean "perhaps"—

A. I. JOSH: I just meant—

MOLLY: You just meant to make no demands—*(She kisses him.)* Not quite like your cow, you understand.

A. I. JOSH: I understand all too well, and Ayoun, that's my cow—

MOLLY: Yes, I've heard—

A. I. JOSH: She understands, too. *(Kissing.)*

SCENE: The Last Supper

All on cell phones.

BOYS: We all thought we'd meet for one Last Supper before we all took off. Yeah, it'd be great, but it's not workin' out. That's the way things shake or do not shake out.

A. I. JOSH: I'm meetin' some budds, we talk cowboy talk can't do the dinn. Yeah, it'd be great.

T-MAC SAM: Can't make the bash. Got bidness of a b-ball nature. Yeah, it'd be great.

K-GAR OLLIE: Can't do the do. Soup kitchen, eatin' in. Yeah, it'd be great.

The BOYS speak to us in unison and straight out.

BOYS:
We're not having our Last Supper as One
What we've done together is fin'ly done
No matter how sad that may seem to be
It's the way, it's the way, yes, we'll see

T-MAC SAM:
I'm off to pursue a basketball dream
With a Technicolor Division Three team
The coach there's Chinese and the forward's
    Sioux
They got a big Polish center name of Stashu
They're likin' my Ebony stride 'n glide
I'll soon have my posse and no place to hide
In a year on out I'm in Dee—Vision One
Thinking N.B.A.—No Babies Allowed—
Never you mind, I'll be having my fun
Do I miss my life former in the Sudanese bush?

Yeah, I miss it, can't be helped
Shoved and pushed, I don't miss that—
No, I don't miss that
Guerillas and GO—rillas—yeah, you know
I can't explain, wrap it around my brain
But I sort of do miss that
That THAT that was that

A. I. JOSH: In the old cowboy movies, you see no cowboys
      black
But they were out there in the Wildest of the
      West
Right there in the front and not in the stage's
      back
And not the mediocre ones, but the very best
I may not be understanding this right
But I think what I'm trying to do
Is get back to the time
because I can't go back home
because home is not there
Back to the time when I leaned on Ayoun
When I studied on the side of that four-legged
      teacher
When each of us was just one more creature
That's what I want
That's what I miss
Not a thing more
Just that and this

K-GAR OLLIE: I got to wonder what I'm missing too
All the sounds of a quiet African night
That never was quiet—a lovebird's coo
Could be heard just before a cheetah's bite
I thought of these noises the other morn
As I served up some waffles at Holy Apostles
And some bad-burned muffins, lemon or corn
To the old deaf lady who pushes and jostles

There I was feeding the hungry and lame
And I couldn't I couldn't remember my name
Who was I where was I and how did I get to
    wherever I was
I thought I would faint, my head was abuzz
Then out of the mist, I was eight, I was ten,
Came my NAME!
And my NAME says,
I'm yours 'til Time freezes over
And then it did, Time suddenly froze
With my name locked in ice, my head hit my toes
Someone picked me off the floor,
The dishwasher or stove
And my name was gone again
I thought I heard its rhyme
But, no, it's gone forever.
All melted and lost in the heat of time
And burned lemon muffins
Or maybe corn

BOYS: Return or not, just as the Elders thought. Perhaps next year we'll think again. Perhaps the pull will be so strong. But for now it ought, it needs, to be so long.

AYOUN *is with us.*

AYOUN: The PEN—Ultimate word from a cow with
                     a 'Tude
These Boys will go on politely or rude.
What do I foresee, good fortune or not
My crystal ball broke, cracked in some pot
With lentils, onions, and rice so hot
This much I can tell, they're bright boys,
    they're good
Whatever happens, whatever transpires

They've enriched our lives and lighted our fires
That's all we can ask for, all that we should
The Lost Boys of Sudan
Each each and each is now a man.

THE END.

FIVE FINGERS OF FUNK

Will Power

Music by Will Power and Justin Ellington

The world premier of *Five Fingers of Funk* was directed by Derrick Sanders and opened on October 24, 2008, at Children's Theatre Company. *Five Fingers of Funk* was funded in part by The Joyce Foundation, the Multi-Arts Production Fund of the Creative Capital Foundation, the Ford Foundation, and the National Endowment for the Arts.

CREATIVE TEAM

Vocal arrangements: Keith A. Hale and Jahi Kearse
Scenic design: Brian S. Bembridge
Costume design: Reggie Ray
Lighting design: Thom Weaver
Sound design: Jill BC DuBoff
Dramaturgy: Elissa Adams
Casting: Jim Carnahan
Stage manager: Stacy McIntosh
Assistant stage manager: Devorah Jaffe

CAST

BIG CED	Keith A. Hale
POPPO	Jahi Kearse
RUBY	Traci M. Allen
DP	Namir Smallwood
FALCON	Matt Rein
DR. FUNK, SLIM, SEYMORE, DEACON BROWN, BOOGIE JONES	Edwin Lee Gibson
BIG CED'S MOMMA, DEE DEE, BOOGIE JONES DANCER, DJ 2	Greta Oglesby
FALCON'S PA, MR. SILVERMAN, SQUEEZY FREEZE MANAGER, DJ 1	Steve Sweere
BOOGIE JONES DANCER, DJ 3	Celeste Jones

CHARACTERS

BIG CED

POPPO

RUBY

DP

FALCON

DR. FUNK

SLIM

SEYMORE

DEACON BROWN

BOOGIE JONES

BIG CED'S MOMMA

DEE DEE

BOOGIE JONES DANCERS (2)

FALCON'S PA

MR. SILVERMAN

SQUEEZY FREEZE MANAGER

DJ 1

DJ 2

DJ 3

SONGS

Five Fingers of Funk

In the Weeds

Poppo Strut

Bustin' Out

Slim

Baby

Sneakin' for the Funk

Leave Me

Squeezy Freeze

Bootylicious

Stand Up

Tell You

Hey Y'all!

The Man

Travelin'

2002

You Can't Leave

Boogie Jones What Ya Want?

Relationship Over

Never Walk Alone

Five Fingers of Funk (reprise)

TIME: 1970s

PLACE: anywhere in the USA

++

ACT ONE

Lights up on DR. FUNK, *a mysterious, omnipotent, psychedelic figure
with sun shades, platform shoes, and a large glow in the dark space robe.*

DR. FUNK: Funk upon a time

In the age of afros

The evil Sith Lord, Darth Tricky Dick ruled
  the land

And chaos reigned supreme

As plagues such as racism

Sexism

And way too tight bell-bottoms, destroyed all
  plant and animal life forms

But out of darkness comes light

And amidst the chaos

A brand-new super group was forming

They called themselves

The Five

Fingers

Of Funk!

Lights up on BIG CED, RUBY, POPPO, FALCON, *and* DP—*fourteen-year-old friends and freshmen at Lincoln High School. The group talks while setting up for rehearsal in* BIG CED'S MOMMA'*s garage.*

BIG CED: Man, why we called the Five Fingers of Funk?

POPPO: What? Man, come on, man, it's obvious, why look—we got five members in the band, right?

BIG CED: Right.

POPPO: And five fingers make a hand, right?

BIG CED: Right.

POPPO: So each of us, watch me now I'm about to get deep, each of us represents one finger, see. And a finger by itself it ain't nothin' you dig? But you put five of those fingers together and you got—

DP: A whole hand!

POPPO: That's right Mr. Hand, man! You got a hand. And brother, you can do 'bout anything with a hand. Shake wit' it, eat wit' it, bounce a ball wit' it.

DP: Wipe yo' ass wit' it!

POPPO: Say man, why you gotta' go get nasty?

DP: 'Cause nastiness is the cousin of funk, baby, and *I* am funky.

Poppo (Jahi Kearse), leader of the newly formed Five Fingers of Funk band, convinces the drummer, DP (Namir Smallwood), to enter the big contest at Dee Dee's Nightclub in *Five Fingers of Funk*. Photograph by Rob Levine.

POPPO: Whatever. Look here, I'm talkin' 'bout symbols you understand? And a hand, a hand is like the ultimate sign, the ultimate power in the universe for peace, or to make a fist, and take it to The Man.

FALCON: Power to the people!

POPPO: Right. And that's why we Five Fingers of Funk, ya dig? 'Cause together we everythang, but separate, we ain't nothing.

DP: I like it too 'cause it got that whole karate thing happenin' in it, man, like *(Does his best Bruce Lee imitation.)*. Woooo-aaaah!

POPPO: Ahhhh-yaaa!

DP: Keyyy-yahh! Yeah-yeah-yeah-yeah you have offended my family, and you have offended the Shaolin Temple. Now, you will taste, Five Fingers of Funk! Ooohwahhh!

POPPO: Uuuwahh!

BIG CED: But wait a minute, man, if we Five Fingers of Funk, then who's the thumb man 'cause I don't wanna be no thumb.

POPPO: It don't matter, man, it ain't that specific, shoot, we all Five Fingers of Funk.

BIG CED: Yeah, but I wanna know, man. See 'cause with these things, I'm always in the un-choiciest of positions you understand? And I ain't tryna be like that no more, like when I was in Soda Pop's dance group, we were the Three Funky Pop Tarts and a Toaster, and I had to be the toaster, man I don't wanna be no toaster!

POPPO: Yeah, but it ain't gonn' be like that round here, man.

RUBY: Because we're all equal.

FALCON: That's right.

DP: And you ain't got to be no toaster—you dig?

BIG CED: OK, well then I'm cool, then I'm cool.

POPPO: Cool baby, look so then do we all agree, that we be the Five Fingers of Funk?

> *Tell me—*
> *Who are we*
> *Who are we*

	Are we niggas?
	Are we niggas?
BAND:	*No-no*
	No-no
POPPO:	*We are—*
BAND:	*Five-Fingers-of Funk*
POPPO:	*Sho' ya right!*
	Who are we?
	Now say—who are we
	Now are we colored?
	Are we colored?
BAND:	*Who are we?*
POPPO:	*Yeah*
BAND:	*Who are we?*
POPPO:	*We are one, two, three, four, five,*
BAND:	*Five Fingers of Funk*
	Five Fingers of Funk
	Five Fingers of Funk
	Five Fingers of Funk
	Five Fingers of Funk
	Five Fingers of Funk
	Five Fingers of Funk
	Five Fingers of Funk
POPPO:	*Now when you walk*
	Know who ya walkin' with babe
	And when you talk
	Know who ya speakin' to babe
RUBY:	*'Cause there are those*
	They'll try to get ya!
BIG CED:	*They'll say they're friends*
	But all the while they was underco-va
DP:	*CIA!*
POPPO:	*So if you gonn' love*
	Know who ya lovin' babe

	And ya do the funky chicken
	Know who ya dancin' with babe
RUBY:	*'Cause there are those*
	They'll try to destroy you
BIG CED:	*Put you in a uniform*
	Then they'll deploy you
POPPO:	*And you'll be fightin' out in Vietnam*
BAND:	*Hell no—we won't go!*
	Five Fingers of Funk
	Five Fingers of Funk
POPPO:	*J. Edgar Hoover—or Nixon whoever bring it on*
	I'ma hit cha wit' my
BAND:	*Five Fingers of Funk*
	Five Fingers of Funk
POPPO:	*Now here we are*
	Practice the music
	In this garage
	But soon we gonn' use it
RUBY:	*Let's take it to the man*
	With a slam dunk
BIG CED:	*We gonna hit cha wit' these five-fingers of funk!*
POPPO:	*We are the grooviest band that you know*
	Yeah yeah yeah!
BAND:	*Five Fingers of Funk*
	Five Fingers of Funk
POPPO:	*This funk is twenty times betta' than dope*
	What's the name y'all?
BAND:	*Five Fingers of Funk*
	Five Fingers of Funk!

Blackout. Lights up on BIG CED, RUBY, DP, *and* FALCON *tuning and prepping for rehearsal. A sign flashes "Freshman Year."*

FALCON: Hey you guys, did ya hear that band at Dee Dee's last week?
DP: Who, the A-Side Players?

FALCON: Yeah man, the A-Side Players. They're like so good, man.

RUBY: Yeah their keyboardist is amazing.

BIG CED: And the dude on the bass he can really throw down.

RUBY: And, they even got a horn section.

FALCON: Wow. Maybe one day, I mean, you guys think we'll get to be that good one day?

DP: That good? Shoot, man, we already better. All they got is a little mo' experience 'cause they seniors, that's all they got.

FALCON: You think so?

DP: I know so. Man, look Falcon, we gonn' hit so hard at Dee Dee's nightclub, man, she gonn' put us on the wall of fame, right next to Boogie Jones.

RUBY: But wait, we gotta win the showcase before we get to the wall of fame, DP. So, maybe we should just try and win the showcase first.

BIG CED: Maybe we should try and play in the showcase first. And we gotta make sure we're good before we do. 'Cause see I seen bands get booed off the stage over there, man, and I don't want that to happen to us, you dig?

DP: Yeah I dig, man, so let's stop talkin' and start practicin' then, shoot, let's get to it, what y'all wanna do, man?

RUBY: Well what you got Cedric?

BIG CED: OK, uh check this out, how about this right here.

BIG CED *plays a gritty, mid-tempo groove on the bass.*

DP: Oh I can get with this.

FALCON: Me too man, that's the one we were messing around with last week, right Ced?

BIG CED: Yeah this the one right here. Y'all remember the parts and everythang? Here we go . . .

RUBY, DP, *and* FALCON *join in on their instruments as* BIG CED *begins to sing.*

BIG CED:	*In the weeds*
	Of my mind
DP, RUBY, FALCON:	*Practice in every way we will play*
	Practice and every day we gonna sing
BIG CED:	*I go back*
	To the riots of sixty-nine
DP, RUBY, FALCON:	*Practice so we can take what will come*
	Be prepared for whatever life shoots your way
BIG CED:	*Fires blazin'*
	So I skid under momma's bed
DP, RUBY, FALCON:	*Practice ya scales*
	Work on ya pitch
	Make sure that the world don't get you sick
BIG CED:	*And on the TV—yeah*
	They say there's already eighteen dead
DP, RUBY, FALCON:	*Rework the bridge*
	Structure the rhyme
	Make sure that ya get your butt to rehearsal—on time
BIG CED:	*Well I'm just glad, so glad, so glad, glad*
	That we can jam
DP, RUBY, FALCON:	*Practice we must, get it right today*
	Make the song as strong as it can possibly be
BIG CED:	*Nothin' gonn' happen to me, as long as I'm in the band*
	We are the band, the funky band
	Now uh Falcon, brother would ya play it for me say
	Play me some guitar, and make it scream hey

FALCON *improvises a wailing, distorted guitar solo.*

BIG CED:	*DP man, I know ya got that beat*
	Could ya gimme somethin' loud, that reaches the street man

DP *plays a solo.*

BIG CED: *Ruby on the keys, girl ya sound good to me*
             Now can ya sing somethin' groovy, come on sing
                 lead girl
             Go head Ruby

RUBY *shakes her head no. Enter* POPPO.

POPPO: Ay what's goin' on family?

BIG CED: Hey Poppo.

RUBY: Hey Poppo.

DP: Poppo, what's happenin' man?

POPPO: What's happenin'? Everythang's happenin'. Let me lay it on
    ya—hit me!

The band cuts into a groove. POPPO *begins to strut around the garage,
recounting his recent adventures.*

POPPO: *I was just out there on Central*
             And they was talkin' 'bout our last show
             How we rocked the barb-a-cue
             Who is this new young crew?
             When y'all play again be sure to let us know
             Well then I made my way to Oak Street
             And they was all talking about me
             Say Poppo damn you smooth
             And we like the way the band grooved
             At the talent show outside, the library

Lights on DEE DEE, *owner of Dee Dee's lounge, a popular teenage hangout.*

DEE DEE: No I liked it, I liked it, I did, but y'all got a lotta growin' to
    do. I mean y'all ain't ready for the big time or nothin' like that,
    no offense but . . . Look, when you are ready, come down to my

club, I'm Dee Dee. OK Poppo, hey nice to meet you too, baby.

POPPO:
Everybody now feel it
The funk we can't conceal it
Pretty soon they all gonn' know us
We'll keep it local this year
But I betcha in one year
All around the world we gonn' be famous

Lights on MR. SILVERMAN, *an older man with a razor-sharp wit. He owns Silverman's records, a mom-and-pop store in the neighborhood.*

MR. SILVERMAN: I've never heard of you. The what? Who? Well do you have a record? Oh, you're playing outside my record store at the block party. Yeah, I can put a flyer up for you kids, sure. And I'll tell you what. I'll save you a spot on the shelf, how's that?

POPPO:
Everybody wanna shake my hand
Everybody wanna hear my band
Everybody tryna figure out where we play next

Lights up on SEYMORE THE JUNKIE, *the self-appointed music critic and naysayer on the block.*

SEYMORE: I heard y'all last week, man, y'all was terrible! You call that music? Well if you tryna improve, you got a loooong way to go, god damn, I might not even live that long. 'Cause y'all some ole' want-a-bees man, wit' a corny ole' name like—

POPPO *tries passing out flyers to people in the neighborhood.*

POPPO:
Five fingers of Funk!—All right y'all
We got a show, hope you can come, Tuesday y'all
I promise we're worth your while
And that ain't no jive
Now gimme five

> *On the black hand side*
> *My band is like the coolest*
> *And the folks is wonderin' how we do this*
> *But magic can't be explained*
> *And the funk it can't be tamed—*

SEYMORE THE JUNKIE: Y'all lame!

POPPO: *Soon we'll be number one*

DEE DEE: Keep practicin'

POPPO: *And forever have big fun*

MR. SILVERMAN: I'll be listenin'

POPPO: *We are the Five Fingers of Funk!*

Exit DEE DEE, MR. SILVERMAN, *and* SEYMORE THE JUNKIE. *Scene shifts back to the band rehearsing in the garage.*

POPPO: So yeah, I passed out flyers to damn near everybody, man, and like the whole neighborhood is commin'.

FALCON: Tuesday?

POPPO: Tuesday six o'clock the block party. Man, it's gonn' be super live.

FALCON: Well do we get a sound check this time? 'Cause, Poppo, when we don't sound check, man, sometimes the amps they feed back during the show, and it sounds bad, man.

POPPO: Naw, naw, naw, don't worry about that, we sound great, let's just meet there outside Silverman's about a quarter to six. And here, here's the set list.

POPPO *passes out the set list to everybody. The band looks it over.*

DP: Say Poppo, man, this is cool, man, but we was diggin' on some a' Big Ced's music before you came, and like we should work some of that into the set, you know?

BIG CED: Naw, naw, DP, I don't wanna be no songwriter. I'm a bass player, and that's more than enough for me.

FALCON: Your songs are cool though, man.

DP: They're super cool, man.

RUBY: Funky grooves from the cutest, coolest bass player around.

BIG CED: Wow, thanks, Ruby.

RUBY: Don't mention it, Cedric.

DP: Aw look the love birds, the funky love birds. Hey, that could be the title to a new song.

POPPO: Ay, Ay, listen y'all I almost forgot. You know I've been thinkin'. Since I, Poppo, am your leader—

DP: We know you the leader, Poppo, what's the point, man?

POPPO: The point, DP, is that I, moi, your leader, has yet to lay down the rules.

DP: Rules? What kinda rules?

POPPO: Rules, man, like, rules, like don'ts and dos, you dig?

DP: Naw, man, I don't dig, 'cause DP ain't into rules. Besides, we got enough rules at school, man.

RUBY: No chewing gum in the hallways.

BIG CED: No food or drink in your locker.

FALCON: No meandering between classrooms.

DP: No kissing, no necking, no hickey-ing.

FALCON: No daydreaming.

RUBY: No dreaming period.

DP: And they ain't made it a rule yet, but they be puttin' pressure on me to cut my natural, man! My teacher say she 'fraid I'm tryna be like Huey P.—Huey P.? Man, I ain't no revolutionary, I'm only in the ninth grade! Dang, man, why they got so many rules?

RUBY: Why you think DP? They got rules 'cause they want me and you to conform.

FALCON: And become part of the high school system, which trains us to be part of "The System."

POPPO: But we Five Fingers of Funk!

RUBY: So we ain't goin' for it!

FALCON: 'Cause this is 1972.

DP: And we bustin' out!

BAND: *Bustin out-aaay*

Bringing this funk to you-aaay

Showin' out-aaay

The Freshmen, we are cool-aaay

Ready to groove-aay

Ready for high school-aay

Here we go

Ya might think we are fools

But even though

We still are virgins-we're bustin' out

POPPO: Alright alright forget the rules, forget the rules.

DP: Yeah, we don't need no rules, man, now let's jam.

POPPO: Yeah, OK, let's do it. But before we do, Big Ced, can you lend me like fifty cent?

BIG CED: Pizza at Ralphie's?

POPPO: Pizza at Ralphie's. *(Big Ced hands Poppo two quarters.)* Yeah, thanks, man, and uh, and if anybody wants to come with me to Ralphie's, after rehearsal, well that would be cool too.

DP: Hey that sounds cool, man, yeah, but I can't today.

BIG CED: Me neither, man. But why don't we go after the gig on Tuesday.

POPPO: Yeah, alright, sounds good to me.

FALCON: Ralphie's it is.

DP: Ralphie's it is then.

BIG CED: Ralphie's!

RUBY: You guys know I've never been to Ralphie's?

POPPO: Are you serious?

DP: Like for reals? But—but that's where everybody go, Ruby, I mean how else can you find out what's happenin'?

POPPO: Yeah, like I go there to get material for new songs.

DP: You go there to look at girls.

POPPO: That too. Man, did you see Dorinda last week? Damn, that girl is superfine, man.

BIG CED: Hold up, why you ain't never been to Ralphie's, Ruby?

RUBY: I'm not allowed to go past Baker Street. It's the wrong side of town.

DP: Wrong side of town? What you talkin' 'bout, man, Ralphie's right there in the neighborhood.

RUBY: Yeah, well, I can't go down there. I hate it, I always miss everything.

POPPO: Ay well, maybe it's for the best, Ruby. There are some shady types on the west side. Like even today—

Band switches to a slower "pimped out" groove. Lights up on POPPO *walking down the street.* SLIM, *a shadowy figure with a green suit and a pair of spit-shine shoes, approaches* POPPO *as he turns a corner.*

SLIM: Say brother
                         What it is?
                         Dig this

                         I got somethin', better then a woman's kiss
                         Tasty like a bowl of grits, with sausage on the side

                         Plus why walk when you can slide
                         And we all gonn' die
                         So why not enjoy the ride, and that ain't no jive,
                              brother

                         And hell, I'll throw the first one in for free
                         Aw what the hell first two bags on me

                         Wait-wait-wait don't go . . . baby I can dig that
                         But how would you know until you try
                         Plus all your heroes get high, man

                         Look at Sly, Jimi, Santana, Miles Davis
                         They couldn't get funky without that supply
                         Dig it—when they partake, what they create gets
                              more intense
                         And like if Jimi was Spider Man, it's like heroin

would be his Spidey sense—you dig?—
tingle tingle

So what he died, so what

Look, man,
I'm just tryna help you reach your full potential
I mean do you wanna be just good, or do you wanna
be monumental?
Come on brother, don't you wanna know what they
know
Feel what they feel
Have what they have
The clothes, the cars, the girls . . .

Alright, alright, yeah, I see
Hey well, when you change ya mind, brother, you
know where to find me, right here
And if I ain't here, just ask for Slim
OK Popp—oh Poppo, hey you Doreen's boy, huh?

Well I'm Slim ya new friend, baby
Yeah OK, OK right on my man
Power to the people

Exit SLIM. *Cross-fade back to band. Enter* BIG CED'S MOMMA, *a nurturing, hard-working woman with stress in her eyes.* BIG CED'S MOMMA *opens the door at the top of the stairs that leads to the garage.*

BIG CED'S MOMMA: Cedric! Cedric!

BIG CED: Uh yes, Momma?

BIG CED'S MOMMA: Baby, do y'all want something to eat down there? Y'all been practicin' so long, ya must be hungry.

BIG CED: Oh yeah, Momma, I am kinda hungry.

POPPO: Hey, man, can your momma make me somethin' too? I'm starvin'.

BIG CED: Oh yeah uh-hey momma, can Poppo eat somethin' too?

BIG CED'S MOMMA: Of course, baby, I got more than enough for everybody. DP, Falcon, Ruby?

DP, FALCON, RUBY: Yes, Ms. Williams?

BIG CED'S MOMMA: Do y'all want something to eat?

RUBY, FALCON, *and* DP *shake their heads no.*

BIG CED: Uh, Momma, just me and Poppo wanna eat.

BIG CED'S MOMMA: OK, baby, well I'll bring somethin' down to y'all in a minute.

BIG CED: Thanks, Momma.

POPPO: Thanks, Ms. Williams.

Exit BIG CED'S MOMMA.

POPPO: So look here y'all, I say it's time we go higher, now what y'all say? Like are y'all ready to sign up at Dee Dee's?

DP: We gonn' win at Dee Dee's!

POPPO: That's right, DP.

DP: Right on, Poppo, give me five, man.

POPPO *and* DP *slap five.*

BIG CED: Wait a minute, man, I don't know if we ready for all that.

FALCON: I agree man. We should wait till we have some stronger songs.

POPPO: Say what? Come on, man, we got plenty of strong songs.

DP: That's right!

POPPO: And I got the perfect one to start with, when we make our debut at Dee Dee's. Check it out, it's somethin' I've been workin' on, y'all ready, y'all ready for it? It goes like this—

> *Ah ah*
> *Uw ba-by*
> *Ah ah*
> *Uw babe*
>
> *Ah ah*

Uw ba-by
Ah ah
Uw babe

Ah ah
I'm feelin' lonely
Ah ah
Need ya today
See I'm rich and horny
Ah ah
And you wanna play
So come to my mansion-baby
Ah ah
Use the phone in my car
Ah ah
My name is Poppo-honey
Ah ah
And I'm a star
Come on girl—

BAND: *Ah-ah-ah-ah-ah-ah-ah-ah-ah-ah-ah-ah babe...*

POPPO: Wuuw, that was the funk right there!

BIG CED: Five Fingers of Funk.

RUBY: Today, Cedric's Momma's garage. Tomorrow, first prize at Dee Dee's—

POPPO: And the next day, the whole motha' funkin' world, you dig?

FALCON: And the day after that, we take it to outer space.

POPPO: Say what?

FALCON: Outer space man. Space is the final frontier of funk!

POPPO: Falcon, I love you, man, but you gotta ease up on them sci-fi conventions.

FALCON: I can't miss my sci-fi, man. Sci-fi and funk, that's what I live for.

DP: Yeah, funk is the way, man, no doubt, but we can only get so funky with them corny lyrics you be singin', man.

POPPO: Ay lay off, DP, shoot, I'm a poet and everybody know it.

DP: I don't know it, man, shoot.

BIG CED: Ay don't be puttin' Poppo down, man. Ay I liked them lyrics, man, I thought them lyrics were good.

DP: What? Come on, Big Ced, man, you got way better lyrics, like, what about that one you was doin' earlier—that's the funk right there.

POPPO: So what was y'all doin'?

BIG CED: Aw nothin', man, we was just messin' 'round you know. Nothin' compared to your song—you got the funk!

POPPO: I know that's right.

DP: Puh-lease.

POPPO: So what you sayin', DP, huh? You sayin' you can write somethin' better than me?

DP: My grandma can write somethin' better than you.

BIG CED: DP, stop bein' so mean, man.

DP: But it's the truth!

BIG CED: We don't need the truth if it's mean.

DP: The hell we don't.

RUBY: Well, Poppo, you wanna know what I think?

POPPO: Not really. Alright, y'all, I gotta go. See everybody tomorrow, same time same channel.

BIG CED: Oh I thought you was stayin' for dinner?

POPPO: Naw, I gotta get to where I'm stayin' tonight, uh after I grab a slice at Ralphie's, and catch up with Dorinda.

DP: You got no chance with Dorinda.

POPPO: We'll see. Later, y'all.

FALCON: Bye, Poppo.

DP: Later, Poppo *(Under his breath.)* you non-poetic son of a . . .

Exit POPPO.

DP: Ay, Ced, you mind if I stay here and jam a little bit?

BIG CED: Don't you gotta pick up your grandma?

DP: Yeah, but I got some time before I need to be there.

FALCON: Oh and me too, can I stay too? I got about like fifteen more minutes.

BIG CED: Yeah, y'all, hey let's hang out. Ruby, you in?

RUBY: I'd love to, Cedric, but I gotta get goin'. Y'all know my daddy don't play.

DP: Uww I know huh Deacon Brown.

Enter DEACON BROWN, *a tall, intimidating man. He paces back and forth behind* RUBY, *staring her down while holding a belt in preparation for the whipping.*

DEACON BROWN: And The Lord say
You shall have no other gods before me.
And The Lord say
I, The Lord your God am a jealous God.
You can't serve two masters, follow him or follow
     death.

Satan tryna kidnap you, girl. Wanna take you
down to hell

And you keep lettin' 'im in
In the form of a pair a' pants
And you let him in
When you smile at some fat boy after school—ha!

So God say,
He say, "Deacon, keep your daughter from the
     devil"
So I've gotta beat ya
'Cause I love ya, I love my little Ruby yeah

DEACON BROWN *raises his belt and comes down hard across* RUBY's *back.*
Exit DEACON BROWN.

DP: Uww Deacon Brown, he scares me, man.

RUBY: Yeah, he is kinda strict.

DP: He stricter than strict, like, I don't even know how you get to
    practice, Ruby!

RUBY: I gotta sneak, DP, shoot I be—

> Sneakin' for the funk
> Sneakin' to play the funk
>
> Don't want my Daddy to know
> He think I'm with my Girlfriend Flo
> Studying the bible
>
> Oh hell no
> I'm sneakin' for the funk
> Sneakin' 'round for the funk
>
> Hope Daddy don't suspect
> That the religion I inject
> Into the cranium
> Come from the funky drum
> The foundation of funk

BAND:
> Sneakin' for the funk
> Sneakin' 'round for the funk

FALCON:
> My Pa he wants to know

Enter FALCON'S PA, *a blue-collar, union factory worker.*

FALCON'S PA:
> Boy, why you like this music so?
> Do you know gosh darnit who you are?
> What the hell you doin' with that guitar?
>
> Now you turn it off right now
> It's time for you and Beth to go to bed
> And if I catch ya playin' that music again
> That guitar's gettin' smashed on your head

Exit FALCON'S PA.

FALCON:
> So now

I just
Pretend
"It was a phase that I was in"
My Pa, he seems, so pleased
That I'm cured of this disease
So now I'm—

BAND: *Sneakin to the play the funk*
Sneakin' for the funk

BIG CED: *Gotta play the groove*
The thang that makes the people move
That's how things will improve . . . through the funk!

RUBY: *But I still can be your girl*
Your pretty pretty pretty pretty girl

FALCON, DP, BIG CED:
And she still will be your girl!

RUBY: *With roses in my hair*
And a pretty blue dress to wear
I'll always be polite
Daddy, I never stray from sight
But somewhere down
down in my dir-ty soul
I can't resist
My body lose control

Oh when it kiss me
When funk hit me
If it's wrong don't wanna be right

And just like this funky music, it make me feel-
alright
So I'll be

BAND: *Sneakin', for the funk*
Sneakin'
Sneakin'
Sneakin'

Lights fade to black. Sign flashes "Sophomore Year." Lights up on SLIM *and* POPPO *in the street.*

SLIM: *They called her insane, but she flipped the game—*
                              your momma
                         Tried to keep her down, like the other hoes—but not
                              your momma

                         She had no pimp, did it on her own
                         They called her the gangsta' bitch
                         Say she would not stop, workin' the block
                         Until she filthy rich

                         I owe it to her, everything I know
                         I learned from your momma
                         And hey I just wish, that you could've known . . .
                         your momma

POPPO: Slim, did she love me?

SLIM: Of course she did. A mother can't help but love her son.

POPPO: Then why did she have to leave?

SLIM: I don't know young brother. I ask the same question
    sometimes.

POPPO: But I wanna know why. Slim, I wanna know.

                         Tell me why she got ta leave me
                         Tell me why she got ta go
                         I was always on the lookout
                         At the window in the Foster home

                         Maybe she bring me some candy
                         Buy me them new roller skates
                         Maybe she'll show up at Dee Dee's
                         Maybe she'll come hear me play

                         I oh I I want to strangle my momma
                         Oh Oh Oh momma Oh momma
                         Wait till I get my hands on my momma
                         Tell me why she got ta leave me

SLIM: Say, Poppo, uh, how's the band, man?

POPPO: Oh everything's everything, you know.

SLIM: But y'all still ain't won at Dee Dee's though.

POPPO: Not yet.

SLIM: Y'all get there one day. Say, when you go to rehearsal today. On your way can ya drop somethin' off for ya best friend?

POPPO: What's that?

SLIM: Oh just a package of this n' that. Here's the address. Make sure you give it to Shay Shay. You do that, you got fifty bucks commin' your way.

POPPO: Naw that's alright, Slim.

SLIM: Aw come on, man, shoot they gonn' be callin' *you* Slim if you don't start eatin' somethin'. You livin' here you livin' there no place a' your own. And how you gonn' be the leader of a band playing soul with them raggedy-ass clothes? But see now if you had some money, that could answer your woes. And I'm tryna place this green, in between and betwixt your fingertips. Now gimme some skin on that, my man.

POPPO: Ay, Slim, I appreciate that, but I can't . . . I mean how can you do this, man?

SLIM: Ain't nothin' to it but to do it, young blood. Check it out—

> I'll throw the first one in for free
> Aw what the hell, first two bags on me

That's my rap. And I was tryna get you hooked, brother man. But now, since we really are friends, and your Momma Doreen was so special to me, I'm tryna bring you in on the business end, dig?

POPPO: I don't know.

SLIM: Look, it's on the way to band practice, my man. It's like I ain't askin' you to make no detour. Just on your way drop this off to sista Shay Shay. Come on, brother.

POPPO: I . . .

SLIM: Fifty dollars, black man. If not for you, then for your band, think of what the band could do with fifty dollars.

POPPO: Alright, since it's on the way . . . I guess I can do that. But only this one time, you dig?

SLIM: I dig it, man, you know I understand. And here, take this for yourself.

SLIM *passes* POPPO *a fifty-dollar bill.*

POPPO: Thanks, man.

SLIM: Ay nothing to it, young blood. I'm just lookin' out for you.

POPPO: Right on, man.

SLIM: Right on, brother. Say, Poppo, remember

> The people
> United
> Will never be defeated

Lights out on SLIM *and* POPPO. *Scene shifts to* BIG CED'S MOMMA *and* BIG CED *sitting at the kitchen table.* BIG CED'S MOMMA *sips a beer.* FALCON *and* RUBY *can be seen downstairs in the garage, awaiting* BIG CED's *return.*

BIG CED'S MOMMA: How's it goin in the garage, Cedric? Y'all havin' lots of fun?

BIG CED: Oh yeah, yeah, it's great, momma. (*Beat.*) Can I go back downstairs now?

BIG CED'S MOMMA: In a minute. Stay here with me for a little while longer.

BIG CED *sits next to* MOMMA.

BIG CED: We all real happy, you know, that you let us be down there.

BIG CED'S MOMMA: Well, your daddy ain't usin' it no more so. You think your friends might want something to eat?

BIG CED: Um, I don't know, I can ask Falcon and Ruby. DP and

Poppo ain't here yet I don't think.

BIG CED'S MOMMA: Well ask them if they wanna stay for dinner.

BIG CED: OK, I will.

BIG CED'S MOMMA: You know your daddy used to be down there with his friends, it was their place for good times too. And just like I do with y'all, I'd bring them food so they wouldn't starve to death. Your daddy especially, Cedric. He was so damn skinny. Huh, I betcha he's somewhere now, starvin'. Anyway . . .

BIG CED: You OK, Momma?

BIG CED'S MOMMA: Same old thing. I tell you, if I didn't have a son to provide for, I would tell all them pecker woods at work where to . . . Yeah, I'm OK. Thanks for caring, baby. Now you go on downstairs and have some fun.

BIG CED: OK, momma, I will.

BIG CED kisses his mother on the cheek and heads down the stairs leading to the garage. As he descends the stairs, enter DP, wearing a bodacious red, white, blue, and polka-dot uniform.

DP: Hey what's happenin', y'all?

BIG CED: Hey, DP! Ay wait a minute, man, what's up with them new threads you got on?

DP: I was 'bout to tell y'all. Check it out. You are lookin' at the newest employee of Squeezy Freeze, can ya dig it?

BIG CED: Wooo you gotta job?

DP: $1.25 an hour. Every Saturday and Sunday, and a few evenin's when I can get 'em.

BIG CED: Aw that's cool, DP.

FALCON: Yeah, and I like their ice cream, man, especially the triple chocolate with the big chunks.

BIG CED: Yeah, but what about they Cherry Pistachio though, uw I love they Cherry Pistachio.

RUBY: But, DP, I thought you wasn't down with authority, so how you gonn' hold down a job?

DP: I don't know, I guess I gotta figure it out.

BIG CED: When you start?

DP: I started already, yesterday was the first day, the boss man led
me through like orientation and what not.

Lights up on the SQUEEZY FREEZE MANAGER. *An overactive, blond-
headed man, he wears a smile that's way too bright.*

SQUEEZY FREEZE MANAGER:

> *Ice Cream, that's what we do here*
> *We give sweetness out all year*
> *Plus onion rings and egg creams*
> *And Rick will show you the slurpy machine*
> *And hot dogs, are frozen in the rear*

Now Dennis, you must have questions on your first day.
I see. You wanna' know when you'll be paid.

> *Well, checks are cut on Mondays*
> *But that's not what I'm talking about*
> *At Squeezy Freeze, we take America's problem and*
> *   scoop it out!*
>
> *Just think, if every dame and every fellah*
> *Came together, like chocolate and vanilla*
> *There'd be no awful marching,*
> *No picketing, no rioting*
> *'Cause everyone would be eating yummy ice cream!*
> *   Oh*
>
> *I scream*
> *I scream*
> *We all scream for ice cream*
>
> *Now tuck your shirt in please*
> *And let's serve some ice cream*
>
> *Everyone is welcomed here because we make ice*
> *   cream*
> *But no di-sheekeys allowed in here*

While you scoop the ice cream

*Butter Pecan? Two scoops? Sir, he'll get your ice
cream*

*Good now Dennis but don't say "cool," unless we're
talking ice cream*

*Howdy ma'am, evening sir, Dennis will get your ice
cream*

*And no slang like "I dig it" unless you're digging out
ice cream*

I scream
I scream
Everyone wants ice cream
I scream
I scream
The whole world loves ice cream
Ice cream!

Exit SQUEEZY FREEZE MANAGER.

RUBY: So you gonn' clean up the act, DP? Cut your afro and
everything?

DP: For Squeezy Freeze? Hell no. Shoot, first and foremost I'm a
drummer, I'm the drummer for Five Fingers of Funk.

RUBY: Go 'head wit' your bad self, DP.

DP: Yeah and yeah, ain't nobody gonn' tell me what to wear and how
to dress. In fact, y'all can come by anytime y'all want, and as
long as my manager ain't around, I'm givin' out free ice cream to
everybody.

BIG CED: For reals?

DP: For reals.

BIG CED: Aw that's cool.

FALCON: Wait, DP, that's like stealing, man.

DP: No it ain't.

FALCON: Yes it is, man, I mean if you don't pay for it.

DP: Well everybody don't get an allowance like you, Falcon.

FALCON: OK, hey you're right. Sorry, man.

DP: Damn right you sorry.

Enter POPPO.

POPPO: Hey y'all, even when I'm late I'm on time—what's happenin', family?

BIG CED: What's goin' on, Poppo?

RUBY: Hey, Poppo.

DP: Ay, Poppo man, like if I can get here with all the stuff I gotta do—school, homework, take care of my grandma, and now a job, then I know you can get here, man.

POPPO: I'm here, DP, so relax, baby.

DP: I mean get here on time, man. In case you forgot, we got a show this Friday at Dee Dee's, and I want to win this one for a change, man.

POPPO: Well let's stop talking and start practicin' then. But before we do, I wanna' have a little Five Fingers of Funk meeting.

DP: A what? A meeting? Aw, man, come on.

POPPO: The first order of business, we need a treasurer.

FALCON: I'll do it.

POPPO: It's done. Now, second order of business. Treasurer, can you please report on how much we have in our treasury?

FALCON: Uh, OK, let's see.

FALCON *reaches for a slightly rusted soup can filled with one-dollar bills.*

FALCON: Well if we add the gig—does this include the show at the library?

BIG CED: Yeah, and the one at the cultural center. What you got right there, that's everything.

FALCON: Alright then we have . . . twenty-seven dollars.

POPPO: Twenty-seven? That's it? Wow that's bad, jack, we can't buy nothin' wit' twenty-seven dollars!

DP: But we don't need nothin', man, shoot, all we need is the groove.

POPPO: Yeah the groove is cool, baby, but it's time to spice up the act.

DP: What you mean?

POPPO: I mean, we need to add a little flair, a little flash, you know? Like if we could get like a little smoke machine, that would make our entrances more dramatic, you dig? Then we could get a couple a' them strobe lights, so that during the Funky Robot song we could make the stage look all staccato and stuff. Or, or at least, well how about some costumes or, or how about we put Ruby in a outfit. Somethin' skimpy, but not too ho-ish, you know, somethin' to get the brothers excited.

RUBY: Poppo—

POPPO: Oh come on, do it for the band, Ruby.

BIG CED: You ain't gotta do nothin' you don't wanna do, Ruby.

POPPO: Shut up, Big Ced, what you know?

DP: We don't need no costumes.

POPPO: Just a little cute little outfit, Ruby. Look, I'll buy somethin' for you with my own money, OK, and just try it on, girl. If you don't like it, you ain't gotta wear it, OK?

RUBY: Alright, Poppo, bring it to rehearsal and I'll try it.

POPPO *whips out the dress that he's had in his guitar case the whole time. He passes it to* RUBY.

POPPO: Cool, ay thanks, Ruby, love ya, baby.

RUBY *takes the dress and moves away from the band.*

POPPO: OK, while Ruby is changin' check out these moves I'm working on for the show, check it out, y'all.

POPPO *shows off his dance moves as the band comes in on the instrumental groove, while* RUBY *begins to uncomfortably change in the corner of the room behind an old dresser drawer cabinet. When* RUBY *is*

done changing, she emerges from the corner and walks across the room,
past the band to her keyboard. The band stops playing and stares at her
in silence.

POPPO: Woo look at that! She look great, right? Aw, Ruby, you look
       great, and don't y'all tell me we ain't gonn win at Dee Dee's. We
       guaranteed to win now, and hey I know the perfect song to go
       with that dress, dig, let's do Bootylicious.

DP: Aw do we have to?

POPPO: Come on, man, wit' that dress we got a number one hit
       automatic, baby. Let's do it!

BIG CED: OK, alright.

                  Boo-ty-licious
                  Boo-ty-licious

                  Boo-tylicious
                  Boo-tylicious
                  Boo-tylicious yeah

POPPO: *Booty!*

BAND: *Shake*
                  Shake-shake-shake-shake-your booty
                  Shake shake shake-shake-shake-shake-that booty

                  Shake
                  Shake-shake-shake-shake-your booty
                  Shake shake shake-shake-shake-shake-that booty

RUBY: *I like to shake my booty!*

BIG CED: *Shake it girl*

RUBY: *I really like to shake my booty!*

POPPO: *Ow!*
                  When ya shake your booty child
                  Movin' across the dance floor
                  I like the way it's groovin' child
                  Ya booty straight drivin' me wild
                  Come on girl!

BAND: *Shake*

> *Shake-shake-shake-shake-your booty*
> *Shake shake shake-shake-shake-shake-that booty*
>
> *Shake*
> *Shake-shake-shake-shake-your booty*
> *Shake shake shake-shake-shake-shake-that booty*

RUBY: *I really like to shake it*

BIG CED: *Oh girl*

RUBY: *I really, really like to shake it*

POPPO: *Ow child, shake that butt-ow!*

RUBY: *My-my-my-my-my booty!*

Enter BIG CED'S MOMMA *at the top of the stairs.*

BIG CED'S MOMMA: Cedric! Cedric!

BIG CED: Uh hold on, y'all.

The band stops playing.

BIG CED: Yes momma?

BIG CED'S MOMMA: What y'all playin' down there?

BIG CED: Uh nothin', we just practicin', tryin' out a new song.

BIG CED'S MOMMA: Well try another song.

BIG CED: Yes ma'am.

BIG CED'S MOMMA: Anyway, I need some help up here.

BIG CED: OK, I'm commin' right now.

BIG CED'S MOMMA: No, send Ruby. I wanna' talk to Ruby.

BIG CED: OK, momma. Ruby, she wanna' talk to you.

RUBY: Alright.

RUBY *climbs the stairs into the kitchen, where* BIG CED'S MOMMA *is busy preparing a meal.*

RUBY: Ma'am?

BIG CED'S MOMMA: Ruby, you—Ruby, my God child, what they got you wearin'?

RUBY: Huh? Oh this is an outfit Poppo got me. We're tryna spruce up the act a little bit.

BIG CED'S MOMMA: And this dress, if I can even call it that, it's gonna spruce up the act?

RUBY: I—I guess so.

BIG CED'S MOMMA: *(Sigh.)* Here, Ruby, take this bowl; help me snap these peas, child.

RUBY: Yes ma'am.

RUBY *and* BIG CED'S MOMMA *peel peas together.*

BIG CED'S MOMMA: Ruby—

> *If you*
> *Gotta rock that boat*
> *So your*
> *Own boat can float*
> *Then them*
> *Mens best learn to row*
>
> *You can't dim*
> *Ya own light*
> *You need it to sail*
> *Through the night*
>
> *If they*
> *Crack the whip, and you pull*
> *Then you'll*
> *Slave like that mule—yes ya will*
> *But you're*
> *A queen girl, not a tool*
> *Ya gotta do*
> *What's right*
> *For you*
>
> *Better stand up!*

Oh—Stand up!—Come on child
Stand up
Just try and just try and stand!—oh girl

'Cause when ya stand
Then the world
Is made right
Oh oh oh oh—oh right!

RUBY: *But, ma'am, I*
Don't mind tryin' it on
And maybe we
Could win if I have it on
And he's the leader
Of Five Fingers of Funk

So shouldn't I do
Just what he wants?
There ain't no back talkin', where I'm from

BIG CED'S MOMMA: *Now you listen here child*
Until ya take
Your first little steps

RUBY: *Ya really think that I should try and stand?*

BIG CED'S MOMMA: *In the direction*
That de-mands respect

RUBY: *The way I am right now it's not so bad*

BIG CED'S MOMMA *Then you'll never*
Know what you've missed

RUBY: *Though I must admit a part*

BIG CED'S MOMMA: *A part a'*

RUBY AND MOMMA: *me—you*
Gets buried deep

It's time for Ruby—yeah
To be complete

BIG CED'S MOMMA: *What ya wanna do is stand up!—Oh*

RUBY: *Ya think I should stand up!*

BIG CED'S MOMMA: *Hoh yes, child, ya gotta stand up!*

Stand up, stand up—stand!
Hoh yeah
'Cause when ya stand
Then the world is made right

See when ya stand
Then the world
Is made right

I think I can take it from here. Thanks for helpin', Ruby. And you
know you can stay for dinner anytime.

RUBY: Thanks, Ms. Williams. Thanks a lot.

RUBY *heads back downstairs. Lights out on* BIG CED'S MOMMA. RUBY
enters the garage. FALCON, BIG CED, DP, *and* POPPO *are engaged in
a laugh.*

DP: Nah-nah it was cool, but I think Falcon was goin' too fast on that
bridge.

FALCON: I know I was, I'm sorry, you guys. I think I do that 'cause I
really wanna get to the vamp, you know?

DP: I hear you, man, but when we in the bridge, we gotsta stay in the
bridge, you dig?

RUBY: Hey, you guys, if you don't mind I'd rather take this off right
now.

POPPO: The outfit? What you look sexy, girl, what's the problem?

RUBY: I don't wanna wear it, that's all.

POPPO: But I spent almost fifty dollars on that dress, man, look them
is real fake rhinestones, man.

BIG CED: She said she don't wanna wear it, Poppo, just take it back to
the store and get a refund.

POPPO: I didn't buy it at no store, and I can't get a refund!

DP: Well that's on you, dolomite, shoot, you the one say she didn't
have to wear it, remember?

RUBY: I'm sorry, Poppo, you know, it's just not me.

RUBY *puts old clothes on over dress.*

POPPO: Well why not? Huh? Why it ain't you? I mean it could be you, why don't ya just give it a try?

RUBY: I did, Poppo, but I don't like it.

POPPO: But I spent all my money on it!

BIG CED: Poppo—

POPPO: Just try, Ruby, damn!

BIG CED: Poppo, cool out, man.

POPPO: Shut up, fat boy, don't tell me to cool out, tell her to cool out and keep that damn dress on! Alright you know what? I see what's going on here. Y'all afraid to win at Dee Dee's, that's what it is. Y'all got that uh, whatchacallit? Inferiority complex, yeah . . . And y'all gonn' be losers like forever, man. So later for you chumps!

BIG CED: Wait, Poppo—

POPPO: Naw.

Exit POPPO.

BIG CED: I'm goin' after him.

DP: What? Why?

BIG CED: 'Cause man, he needs us.

Enter BIG CED'S MOMMA *at the top of the stairs.*

BIG CED'S MOMMA: Cedric, it's dinnertime!

BIG CED: I'm coming, Momma!

DP: Poppo trippin', man.

Exit BIG CED'S MOMMA. BIG CED *goes to the entrance of the garage and peeks his head out, hoping to catch up with* POPPO. *But* POPPO *is long gone.*

BIG CED: Damn. My momma callin' me, we gotta pack it up for today, y'all.

FALCON: Yeah, I gotta go anyway, you guys.

DP: Yeah, me too, man.

BIG CED: Alright then later, y'all.

FALCON: Later.

DP: Catch ya later, my man. (DP *slaps* BIG CED *five.*) See y'all tomorrow. And this Friday at Dee Dee's we gonn' win, man—we can't be beat!

Exit DP *and* FALCON.

BIG CED: Ain't you gotta go too, Ruby?

RUBY: Well believe it or not, my daddy is at a conference. So for once in Lord knows how long I have a little free time.

BIG CED: You mean you ain't gotta bolt outta here?

RUBY: Exactly. So you wanna jam?

BIG CED: What, just me and you?

RUBY: Yeah, just me and you, ain't nobody else here.

BIG CED: That's true. So what you wanna play?

RUBY: I don't know. Anything. How about one of your grooves?

BIG CED: OK, yeah sure.

RUBY: Cedric, how come you never want to play your songs in rehearsal?

BIG CED: Uh well, I don't know, I mean Poppo's the leader, you know, he's the one that's supposed to be out there, not some fat boy. I mean, come on, have you ever seen a band that had a leader that looked like me? I don't think so.

RUBY: Well you could be the first.

BIG CED: Ruby, what you wanna play?

RUBY: You afraid people are going to laugh at you?

BIG CED: No, no, I ain't afraid a' that, I just . . . well maybe.

RUBY: I think your songs are beautiful, Cedric.

BIG CED: Really?

RUBY: Really.

Pause.

RUBY AND BIG CED: OK, let's play.

BIG CED *begins to play a soft, mid-tempo groove.* RUBY *joins in on her keyboard, then begins to sing.*

RUBY:	*How can I tell him?*
	How can I tell him?
	That he means so much to me
BIG CED:	*How can I tell her?*
	And if I tell her
	Will she just laugh
	Then
	Run
	From me?
	Oh, man, I might make this wrong
RUBY:	*We've been friends so long*
BIG CED:	*And if I tell her*
	Will I lose
	My
	Buddy?
RUBY:	*Ruby, don't be shy*
	'Cause if you like this guy
	You gotta be strong
	Now go on
	Tell him
BAND:	*Tell him!*
RUBY:	*got so much emotion balled up inside*
BAND:	*Tell him*
RUBY:	*The feelings I got for you, Cedric*
	How can a sista' girl even hide?
BAND:	*Tell her!*
BIG CED:	*I dream about*
	Walking with ya, my hand in your hand
BAND:	*Tell her!*
BIG CED:	*You be my woman*

And I'd be your big, cuddly lover man

How can I tell you
What if I tell you
That you're al-ways
On
My
Brain

RUBY: *How can I tell you*
Wish I could tell you
That I want you
As
My
Main man

BAND: *Tell him!*

RUBY: *I love the funk*
And it's time for us to get funky

BAND: *Tell her!*

BIG CED: *I'm addicted to your love*
Like a strung out heroin junkie

BAND: *Tell him!*

RUBY: *I am a seagull*
And you are my sand

BAND: *Tell him!*

RUBY: *I can fly around all day*
But I ain't home till I reach your land

BAND: *Tell her!*

BIG CED: *I need me some Ruby*
'Cause I'm so stiff and robotic

BAND: *Tell her!*

BIG CED: *I'm a fish in your pond, babe—*
And you got me feelin' mighty aquatic

BAND: *Tell him!*

RUBY: *Oh I love me some Cedric*

	He could be my big teddy bear
BAND:	*Tell him!*
RUBY:	*I love you, Cedric*
	And if the band know I don't care

Song ends. RUBY *and* BIG CED *face each other in an awkward silence.*

RUBY: Well, it's been nice jammin' with you, Cedric.

BIG CED: Yeah, you too, Ruby.

RUBY: Yeah, it was nice. *(Pause.)* Well, I guess I'll see you later.

Big Ced: Uh, OK.

Ruby: Bye, Cedric.

RUBY *begins to pack up her things.* BIG CED'S MOMMA *enters at the top of the stairs.*

BIG CED'S MOMMA: Cedric! Dinner's ready!

BIG CED: Commin', Momma.

BIG CED'S MOMMA *descends the stairs.*

BIG CED'S MOMMA: Cedric, did you hear me—Oh. Hey, Ruby.

RUBY: Hello, Ms. Williams.

BIG CED'S MOMMA: Ruby girl, would you like to stay for dinner? I got plenty, you know.

RUBY: No thanks, ma'am, I have to get going.

BIG CED'S MOMMA: OK, baby.

RUBY: Bye, Ms. Williams, bye, Cedric.

BIG CED: Bye, Ruby.

Exit RUBY.

BIG CED'S MOMMA: Cedric, baby, you and Ruby down here by yourselves?

BIG CED: Uh yeah well, everybody else had to leave, so we were just messin' around and stuff. I mean not messin' around like that, but just messin' around like, uh, playin' music and stuff.

BIG CED'S MOMMA: Well I should hope you weren't 'messin' around, Cedric. I like Ruby, but she's not the one for you.

BIG CED: Ma'am?

BIG CED'S MOMMA: Well, she's a nice girl and all but . . . she lies to her daddy and sneaks around behind his back. That's not right, Cedric, and if she does that to him . . . anyway, look it's time for dinner. And you know I don't like when the food gets cold. So come on, let's go.

BIG CED: Yes, momma.

BAND: *Tell her!*

Exit BIG CED'S MOMMA *and* BIG CED. *Scene moves to Dee Dee's lounge. Enter* FALCON, POPPO, RUBY, DP, *and* BIG CED. *They launch into a funky, up-tempo groove. Dee Dee voice-over.*

DEE DEE: Hey, y'all! Welcome to Dee Dee's! Where funkyness is the principality, and dreams become reality.

Now, it's now my pleasure to bring to you a group that's ready to funk the stage. These young funkateers are regulars down here at Dee Dee's. They're in the tenth grade outta Lincoln High. So please put your hands together for the Five Fingers of . . . Funk!

POPPO: What's groovy, y'all? Yeah, baby, dig it, we are Five Fingers of Funk. And I wanna ask y'all one thing right here. Say—

Hey y'all, what's happenin'?
Hey Y'all, what's groovy?
Hey y'all, what it is?—Yeah!
Do y'all wanna party?

Now if ya do
Get on the floor, y'all, and shake that funky thang—
            hey!

	Don't be ashamed, y'all, gotta let it all hang—hey!
	You see a big girl, and she got plenty rump—hey!
	Don't be afraid go ask her to do the bump
	Say—
BAND:	*Hey y'all, what's happenin'?*
	Hey Y'all, what's groovy?
	Hey y'all, what it is?—Yeah!
	Do y'all wanna party?

POPPO *gets the audience to participate.*

BAND:	*Jump back*
	Turn around
	Get that funky thing
	Jump back
	Turn around
	Get that funky thing!
	Jump back
	Turn around
	Get that funky thing
	Jump back
	Turn around
	Get that funky thing!

The band brings the song to a dramatic end. Blackout.

ACT TWO

Lights up on DR. FUNK *in a funktified, meditative trance. Eerie, synthesized sounds linger in the back.*

DR. FUNK:	*Five Fingers of . . .*

Five Fingers of . . .
Five Fingers of Funk . . .

Five Fingers of . . .
Five Fingers of . . .
Five Fingers of Funk . . .

Lights out on DR. FUNK. *Sign flashes "Junior Year." Lights up on* BIG CED, FALCON, RUBY, *and* DP *setting up to rehearse in the garage.*

DP: Man, I can't believe they robbed us, man!

FALCON: DP, that was last spring, man.

DP: I know, but still, Loca-Function? How Loca-Function gonn' beat us, man? OK, OK, Juan is funky, no doubt about that. But them other jokesters, the one with the leopard skin, and the dude that be commin' out with no shirt?

BIG CED: Yeah, he need to put a shirt on.

DP: For real. And you ever smelled that dude? He be smellin' nasty, man, deodorant all caked up under his armpits. Shoot, just 'cause you funky don't make you funky, you dig?

FALCON: Get over it, DP.

DP: But we were robbed! And Falcon, you don't understand the severity of what I'm talkin' 'bout. See we could be like Boogie Jones, man! After he won, he became a shooting star, but he still live in the neighborhood. Man, that could be us, man, but not if we don't win at Dee Dee's, ya dig?

BIG CED: Well, I don't know what else we can do, DP.

DP: Well let's play some a' your songs, 'cause all we ever do is play Poppo's songs. Shoot, I'm surprised we came in second place last time.

BIG CED: Yeah, but see, we took second place for the first time, that proves that we're gettin' better.

DP: Yeah, we gettin' better, but our songs ain't gettin' no better. And like how we gonn' beat all them good bands man if we don't have good songs. Like we need to play your songs, man.

BIG CED: DP, man, how many times have we—look writin' songs and singin' lead, that ain't my job, my job is to make everybody else sound better, that's why I'm a bass player, dig?

DP: No, man, I don't dig. Like you always takin' care of everybody, Ruby, Poppo, your momma, everybody but yourself, man, it's time for you to shine, man! Like if not for you then for the band, do it for the band, man!

Enter POPPO.

POPPO: Hey what's happenin', family?

BIG CED: Hey now, Poppo.

POPPO: Ay what's goin' on, fat man. Hey Falcon, DP, what's happenin', Ruby, wit' yo' foxy self. Girl, someone needs to sop you up with a biscuit, gimme a chance, girl, god damn! What it is everybody?

DP: What's goin' on, Poppo?

POPPO: Oh you know, just doin' my thing in the school and on the streets . . .

FALCON *plays a sustained wah-wah guitar. Scene shifts to* SLIM *and* POPPO *on the street.*

SLIM: Hey Poppo.
              What's goin' down, young brother?
              Do ya got somethin'
              For your best friend? Slim

SLIM *receives money from* POPPO.

SLIM: You short again Poppo. And I'm tryna work with you here, young blood. See 'cause, I promised your momma

              If I ever met you
              I would take

Care
Of her son

Yeah yeah. But you makin' it difficult, brother man.

POPPO: I know, Slim, ay I don't wanna mess with you, man.

SLIM: It ain't me you got to worry about, young blood. See you gotta watch out for Shay Shay. Like when you owe me, you owe her, and that bitch ain't one to mess with I'ma tell ya right now.

POPPO: I know.

SLIM: No, you don't know. See 'cause you ain't seen evil till you seen Shay Shay get ugly.

POPPO: But she's always nice when I make the drop-off.

SLIM: That's 'cause she likes you. But that can change quick, my man, so stop skimmin' off the top.

POPPO: OK, Slim.

SLIM: I'm serious, Poppo. I can only cover for you for so long, man. Shit, you gonn' get me in trouble, and that's a definite no-no, brother.

POPPO: Alright, Slim.

SLIM: Alright. Now I got three packages here for Shay Shay, and these for Baker Street. And try to make it quick, man.

POPPO: But, Slim, I gotta, I gotta get to practice, man.

SLIM: Practice? What do I care about your practice? Now deliver these packages like I say. And hurry up, man.

POPPO: Alright, alright three—

SLIM: Three to Shay Shay and two to Baker Street. Now go on now.

POPPO: OK. Ay, Slim, power to the people, man.

SLIM: Yeah yeah, power to people.

Exit SLIM. *Scene shifts back to the band in the garage.*

POPPO: Yeah, everything is cool. Got my class schedule, my notebook, got my black book for phone numbers, you dig? Look, I already got like three phone numbers from the first day of school! Tell me I ain't super fly.

DP: Man, you ain't super fly.

POPPO: Whatever, DP. You just mad 'cause I get the ladies, and you
   don't. Now, if you want me to hip you to the hustle, baby, I'm
   more than willing to help a young brother out, you dig?

DP: I don't need nothin' from you, man. I got my own job, I'm a
   grown man.

POPPO: Liftin' boxes all day, you call that a job? Sound like servitude
   to me.

DP: You the servant, chump, runnin' packages all over town. Man,
   you ain't nothin' but a gopher with a perm.

The band laughs. RUBY *continues to laugh after the others have stopped.*
POPPO *menacingly approaches* RUBY. *She shrinks.*

POPPO: You think that's funny, Ruby? Huh?

RUBY: No, no, it's not funny, Poppo, it's not, I'm sorry.

POPPO: That's right you are sorry. And as for you, DP, yeah I deliver
   stuff for Slim, so what, at least I'm makin' me some money, baby,
   which is more than I can say for all you broke suckers.

DP: Yeah, whatever, man.

POPPO: Yeah whatever is right, chump!

DP: Ay don't call me no chump, man.

POPPO: Why not? That's what you are. Tryna judge what I do, man,
   you can't even hold down a job, like how many times have you
   been fired in the last year alone, man?

DP: So what, at least I'm still workin', most people I know is
   unemployed and can't find a job, but I always find one, so I
   always stay workin'. And my grandma is proud of me, and that's
   all that matters, man.

POPPO: Oh yeah? Well what about the Five Fingers of Funk? What,
   we don't matter no more?

DP: Man, you should ask yourself that question. 'Cause I'm here
   early every day, but you always late, Poppo. And when you get
   here, the first thing you do is brag about your money and all your
   ladies, and that raggedy secondhand Lincoln you got parked

outside. You don't care about the music, you don't care about us, you only out for yourself, and that's how you've always been, man.

POPPO: What? Well let me ask you something then, let me ask all a' y'all somethin'. Who pays for most of the stuff around here, huh? All the equipment repairs, the transportation costs, all of it comes from my pocket. And y'all don't even know what I gotta deal with to get this money in the first place, y'all don't even know, OK? I put my butt on the line everyday for y'all. And this is how you repay me? Talkin' about me? Laughin' at me? Well forget y'all then, it's time to break up the band—it's over!

FALCON: What?

BIG CED: Wait—wait wait a minute.

DP: It's over for you maybe, but not for us, we don't need you, take your money, who cares.

POPPO: Yeah, alright, I'll take the money, but I'm takin' the name too. 'Cause I came up with Five Fingers of Funk, the name is mine, and I'm takin' it with me.

DP: No you not.

POPPO: Well what you gonn' do, nigga'? You gonn' stop me?

DP: Nigga'? Oh hell no you ain't callin' me no nigga', put 'em up, jive turkey!

POPPO: Put 'em up then!

DP *and* POPPO *rush each other.* BIG CED, FALCON, *and* RUBY *break them apart before any punches are thrown. Enter* BIG CED'S MOMMA *at the top of the stairs.*

BIG CED'S MOMMA: Hey, hey what's goin' on down there, y'all?

BIG CED: Oh nothin', momma, we just practicin'.

BIG CED'S MOMMA: Alright, well you know the garage is for music.

BIG CED: OK, momma.

BIG CED'S MOMMA: Alright. Now look, I got some chocolate cupcakes for everybody. And I'll bring 'em down when they're finished.

POPPO: Thank you, Ms. Williams.

DP: Thanks, Ms. Williams.

Exit BIG CED'S MOMMA.

BIG CED: Ay y'all, look, why don't we just start rehearsal. OK?

POPPO: Yeah, OK, yeah, let's start rehearsal, let's do it, let's do uh
The Man, let's do The Man, y'all wanna do The Man? Let's do
The Man.

BIG CED: Alright, let's do The Man. OK, y'all, one, two—

POPPO: Ay ay I count off the band, man, that's my job!

BIG CED: Sorry, man, I was just tryna help.

POPPO: Well don't. OK, here we go, y'all, one, two, three and—

The band hits the groove.

BAND:	*The Man*
	The Man
	The white man!
BIG CED:	*Don't get caught sleepin' with the—*
BAND:	*Man*
	The Man
	The White Man!
RUBY:	*He'll brainwash ya*
BAND:	*The Man*
	The Man
	The cracker, the honkie—The Man

FALCON: Hold up, hold up, you guys, wait a minute.

The band stops.

DP: What? Aw come on, man, why you stop the groove, man!

FALCON: I know, I'm sorry, I'm just . . . I mean I wanna talk to
you all.

DP: What, man?

RUBY: Go 'head, Falcon, what is it?

FALCON: Well it's just, I know The Man is the system, and I'm against the system too, you know, power to the people!

POPPO: That's right!

FALCON: Right, but when we say the white man, I mean, does that mean me too?

BIG CED: No.

DP: Yes!

BIG CED: He ain't part of the system like that.

DP: Yeah he is, I mean kinda, I mean he ain't The Man, but he's still white, which means he gets some privilege, 'cause The Man is white.

BIG CED: But I thought The Man was, was a system?

DP: The Man is a white system, for white people, you dig?

FALCON: But I thought the funk made us all the same?

DP: What? Hell no! Shoot, who told you that, man?

BIG CED: Wait, Falcon's right. We all one, remember, the five fingers of the funk.

DP: Ay, Falcon is cool, man, and we a band yeah, but he's white and I'm black, and we'll never be the same, you dig?

FALCON: Yeah, that's what my Pa says too. That's why he says we have to move.

RUBY: You're gonna move, Falcon?

FALCON: Yeah, I think so. Out to Sheffield I think.

DP: Sheffield?

BIG CED: But if you move out there, how you gonn' still be in the band?

FALCON: I don't know.

DP: Ay well, Falcon, I hope you don't have to move, I mean it won't be five fingers without you, man.

FALCON: Thanks, DP.

DP: But I ain't changin' how I feel though, man—white and black, two different galaxies, and ain't nothin' ever gonn' change that.

BIG CED: Ay can we please get back to the groove? Please?

DP: Yeah, let's get back to the groove.

POPPO: Let's take it from where we left off. OK, here we go, one, two,
three, and—

BAND: *The Man*
                        The Man
                        The White Man
BIG CED: *Only by the hand of a strong—*
BAND: *Black man!*
                        Can we beat The Man
                        The Black man
                        Will beat The Man

RUBY: Wait, hold up, hold up, Hooold up.

(Band stops again.)

DP: What?

RUBY: I don't like these lyrics anymore. I mean, why are we saying
only by the hand of a strong black man? What about all the
strong black women in the struggle?

POPPO: Ruby, girl, shut up wit' all that, damn. *(Poppo tries to start the
song.)* One, two, three—

BIG CED: Wait, wait, man, I think Ruby wants to say something here.

POPPO: What, Ruby, what you wanna say?

RUBY: I wanna say . . . uh . . . I have a song.

POPPO: What?

RUBY: I have a song that I want to sing. And I want to put it in the set.

POPPO: Since when did you become a songwriter?

RUBY: I've always written songs. It's just . . . you don't really know
me. Look, can you at least just listen to it before you say no?

BIG CED: Go 'head, Ruby, do your song.

RUBY: Poppo?

POPPO: Yeah, yeah, go 'head, girl, whatever.

RUBY: Alright, here it goes . . .

> *Travelin' on a road to my heart*
> *Makin' my way with spare parts*
> *Travelin' on this road to my heart*
> *Replacing the piece that was lost*

Everyone
Needs a purpose, babe
Something more than your commands

Don't know mine
But I ain't worried, babe
My feet ready for the sand

Now I used to obey
And believe your every word
When you say I was made from a man's rib—hey
And I respect
That's how ya feel
But it don't mean
But it don't mean
That it's the way that I've got to live—I think I'll go—

Travelin' on a road to my heart
Makin' my way with spare parts
Travelin' on this road to my heart
Replacing the piece that was lost

I've been around so many cold places
I've been threatened with hell fire
But now I see the facade startin' to crack
And you can't hold me back

Travelin' on a road to my heart
Makin' my way with spare parts
Travelin' on this road to my heart
Replacing the piece that was lost

POPPO: Alright, let's take a break.

DP: A break?

POPPO: Yeah, a five-minute break, I wanna talk to Ruby over here in private about this song.

BIG CED: In private?

POPPO: Look, just y'all go over there and talk amongst yourselves, me and Ruby'll just be a minute.

POPPO *takes* RUBY *by the arm and leads her to a private part of the garage.*

POPPO: I'ma let you do your song, but what you gonn' do for me?

RUBY: What you mean?

POPPO: Come on, girl. You know I've been diggin' on you since the first rehearsal. And I know you and fat boy got a little thing for each other, but look here, I'm the real deal, ya understand?

RUBY: Poppo, let go of my arm.

POPPO: Oh sorry, sorry. Look, I dig you, girl, just give me a chance. You know I talk a lot of stuff, but I don't mean all the things I say, not mostly anyway.

RUBY: Poppo, what do you want from me?

POPPO: I want you to like me. And I want us to go out. Yeah, you know, like let's grab a soda at Ralphie's, and get to know each other beyond this little funky garage, you dig?

RUBY: Poppo, I do like you, but not like that.

POPPO: OK, OK, but how do you know, you don't even know me, you don't know the real me.

RUBY: OK, who is the real you then?

POPPO: What? Aw come on, girl, now you gettin' too deep for me, let's go out first, then we can explore all that.

RUBY: Poppo, you are cute but—

POPPO: See I knew you liked me.

BIG CED: Ay Poppo, are we gonna keep rehearsin' or what, man?

POPPO: Hold on now, Fat Albert, me and Ruby talkin'. So after rehearsal, can I buy you a soda or what?

RUBY: Poppo, I . . .

POPPO: Look, I know you like Cedric, but he ain't got no nerve, he's a momma's boy. And if you go with him, you'll always play second fiddle to his momma, trust me on this.

RUBY: But I like Cedric.

POPPO: No you don't. You think you do but you don't. Look, how you gonna like someone that's too scared to like you back? Now, come on, now, I'm askin' you for the third and last time, can I buy you a soda at Ralphie's?

RUBY: OK, fine a soda, but just a soda, 'cause I ain't promisin' you nothin', Poppo. And you should know right now, that I don't put out.

POPPO: That's OK with me, truth be told I'm still a virgin.

RUBY: Huh?

POPPO: Ay y'all, me and Ruby talked it over, and we gonn' add that song to the set.

DP: Say what?

BIG CED: For real?

POPPO: Yeah, yeah, it's sweet you know? And we need some sweetness in the Five Fingers of Funk. In fact, I think Ruby should take an even more active role in songwriting for the band, like she gonn' be my co-writer. Ain't that right, babe?

RUBY: Yeah.

DP: Aw that's cool, that's cool, but now what about Big Ced, can we add some a' his songs too?

POPPO: Well yeah, maybe one day, you know, but for now me and Ruby, we'll write all the songs, OK? So . . . wait (POPPO *checks his watch.*). Aw damn. Ay y'all, you know what? I gotta go run some errands.

DP: Say what? Aw come on, Poppo man, look, you came in super late, and now you 'bout to leave early?

POPPO: Relax, DP.

DP: Man, you relax! Shoot, we tryna win at Dee Dee's, fightin' for our lives up in there, and you gotta go run errands? Man, what kind a' leader are you, man?

BIG CED: DP don't really mean that, Poppo.

DP: Man, how you gonn' say what I mean? Damn, Big Ced, you always tryna make everything right when it ain't. Like why don't you try to be real for a change, and call a spade a spade, you dig?

POPPO: Say look here, I don't know why y'all gettin' all riled up, 'cause I'ma be right back.

DP: Forget you, Poppo man, you phony.

BIG CED: Relax, DP.

DP: Big Ced, shut up, man!

POPPO: I'ma catch y'all later. And Ruby, I'll see you at Ralphie's.

RUBY: Hold up. I'll go with you now; I mean rehearsals almost over anyhow, right?

POPPO: Uh, yeah, yeah, rehearsal is almost—you know what, let's end rehearsal, y'all. I think we all need a breather here, and tomorrow we'll start up again fresh. OK? Alright bye, Falcon, bye, DP. See you later, Cedric.

BIG CED: OK. Bye, Ruby.

Exit RUBY *with* POPPO.

DP: Wait, what the—Big Ced, you better stand up for yourself.

BIG CED: What you talkin' 'bout?

DP: You know what I'm talkin' 'bout, man. I mean you gonn' let 'im just walk out with your girl like that?

BIG CED: She's not my girl. *(Pause.)* Aw man, momma!

BIG CED *tries goes upstairs to speak to his mother.* DP *blocks him at the foot of the steps.*

DP: Wait a minute, where you goin'? Come on, Big Ced, we gotta play, man, we need to play.

BIG CED *pushes past* DP *and heads for the stairs.*

BIG CED: Momma!

Exit BIG CED.

DP: You know what? We ain't gonn' never win at Dee Dee's, man.

FALCON: Yes we will, DP.

DP: Oh yeah? Well how is that when three-fifths of the band is runnin' outta here. I'm tellin' you, we got no chance.

FALCON: Yes we do. Maybe we won't win this Friday, I don't know, but we'll win one of these days.

DP: Yeah, but I don't wanna wait for one of these days, man, I wanna win now.

FALCON: I hear you, man, but—

> *We can't see, what we will do*
> *When we are living in 2002*
> *A long ways away*
> *Will earth fade away*
> *Then we'll keep it funky in space*
> *We'll do the jerk*
> *With Captain Kirk*
>
> *Finding ways to resuscitate*
> *This beautiful nation but some say it's too late*
>
> *Now it's 2002, the fighting has stopped*
> *No wars, no guns, no crooked cops*
> *And everyone will have a pet rock*
>
> *And it will be love*
> *And you'll still play the drums*

So we're here Five Fingers of Funk
We're making rhythms to help people move on
And if one day we stop and we lose
Then kids who live in 2002
Will hear the things that we tried to do
And they'll keep the groove

The song ends. DP *and* FALCON *look at each other. Lights fade to black. Sign flashes "Senior Year." Lights up on* BIG CED *sitting alone in the garage, playing his bass. Enter* DP.

DP: Man, did you hear the news, man? Dee Dee's is closin'!

BIG CED: What?

DP: Closin', outta business, the doors getting shut and everything, man.

BIG CED: But we're in the showcase this Friday.

DP: But now it's gonn' be the last one ever.

BIG CED: Aw man, I thought we had all of senior year to win.

DP: We got less than a week to win. And Dee Dee say this one is gonna be special since it's the last one, so she's invitin' all the bands that ever made it big to be there. I'm talkin' 'bout the A-Side Players, Granny and the Funkatroids, the Flamingos of Funk, and of course Boogie Jones, man, they all gonn' be there, so we gotta win now, 'cause all our heroes gonn' be watchin' us.

BIG CED: Not to mention all our friends.

DP: And everybody from Central and Lincoln High. Like tickets is already sold out!

BIG CED: Wow, this could be our big chance!

DP: Our big break.

BIG CED: Or our big embarrassment. I mean if we mess up, like if I forget a chord change, I mean I'm messin' up in front—

DP: In front of everybody. I know, so we can't mess up, not now, not after four years of practicin', shoot. Everybody at Lincoln excited about graduating, man, our graduation goes down Friday night at Dee Dee's, and we ain't guaranteed no diploma, you dig? So where's everybody at, man?

BIG CED: Uh well, Falcon, I don't know, I guess his bus ain't arrived from Sheffield yet. And Poppo and Ruby, they probably at Ralphie's, sittin' at that table in the back, holdin' each other close, whisperin' sweet nothings to one another while they sip that grape soda. Me and Ruby never did that, but I used to walk her to school sometimes. And I remember sometimes we would—

DP: Hey hey hey, Big Ced, don't do this, man. Like you always get depressed when you start talkin' 'bout Ruby.

BIG CED: I know, but I can't help it. I've tried to get her out of my mind but . . .

Enter POPPO *and* RUBY.

POPPO: Hey family! Say dig on the threads I bought Ruby. And look here, these are the same kind a' shoes Chaka Khan wears in concert. I'm tellin' you, Pam Grier better watch out, 'cause there's a new afro sex kitten on the scene, and her name is Ruby Brown!

RUBY: I'm soul sister number one, ready to stand with my black king and take it to The Man at the same time.

POPPO: Ruby Brown! Wuuu. Ruby, there's nothin' I wouldn't do to keep you, 'cause I love you, I love my little Ruby.

RUBY: Poppo, I . . . Look, I need to talk to Poppo in private.

POPPO: In private?

RUBY: Just five minutes, y'all, please.

RUBY *pulls* POPPO *by the arm to a corner on the other side of the garage.*

RUBY: I've never heard you say that before.

POPPO: Say what?

RUBY: That you love me like that.

POPPO: Well I do. And I don't care who knows it either, 'cause you're mine and I ain't never lettin' you go.

RUBY: Poppo . . . look . . .

I really love the time we spend together
And even though we said it'd be forever
I've
Gotta listen
To my truth

See there's another boy
He knows my heart
And only when I stop playin' the part
Will I
Find
My truth

So I've got to leave you
I've got to leave you
'Cause, honey, if I stay wit' chu
I know
I won't grow

POPPO: *But Ruby . . . what about that coat I bought ya*
What about the things I taught ya
'Bout how to stay alive on these streets
Everything you know you learned from me

What about the strolls we took together
And the promises we made to each other
'Bout how it's always gonna be
You and me

You can't
Leave me
You can't
Leave me!

'Cause if you leave me
Poppo will be so alone

BIG CED: *I've thought about it for far too long*
What the hell did I do wrong?

To lose
The perfect
Girl for me

But I thought she could never really love me
'Cause I was just too fat and sloppy
But maybe
Just maybe
She'll see me

I hope she leave him
I hope she leave him
'Cause if she leave him
This time, I won't say no

BAND: *Leave him*
You should
Leave him
Leave him!

BIG CED: *So I hope she leave him*
I know that's bad
But still I hope she leave him
'Cause maybe if she leave him
My broken heart
Will be whole

So I hope she leave him
POPPO: *Don't leave me baby!*
RUBY: *I've got to leave*
BIG CED: *I hope she leave him*
POPPO: *I'm gonna kill you if you leave*
RUBY: *Honey, I've got to go*
BIG CED: *Ruby, leave him*
POPPO: *Ruby, stay with me girl*
RUBY: *Oh wait . . . I don't know*
BIG CED: *Leave him!*
POPPO: *No, you should stay, baby, stay here, baby, sta-ay!*

RUBY: *No, no, baby, I've got to leave*

BIG CED: *That's right, Ruby, you got ta leave*

POPPO: *Shut up, Big Ced*

BIG CED: *No, you shut up, Poppo!*

RUBY: *Both a y'all be quiet, let me think, no, I've got to go*
                                          'cause

RUBY, POPPO, BIG CED:

                                    If you leave

                                    My heart

BIG CED: *Will be mended*

POPPO: *Will be ended*

RUBY: *Will be whole*

RUBY, POPPO, BIG CED:

                                    If

                                    You

                                    Leave

RUBY: I gotta go, Poppo. I'm sorry.

POPPO: Yeah, me too.

RUBY *turns from* POPPO *and walks to the other side of the room. Enter* BIG CED'S MOMMA *at the top of the stairs.*

BIG CED'S MOMMA: Cedric!

BIG CED: Uh yeah, momma!

BIG CED'S MOMMA: Can you put out the garbage before the garbage men get here? It's Tuesday.

BIG CED: Oh yeah, OK, no problem, I'll do it now.

BIG CED'S MOMMA: Thank you, baby.

Exit BIG CED'S MOMMA.

BIG CED: I gotta take out the garbage, y'all, I'll be right back.

RUBY: Uh, Cedric, can I go with you?

BIG CED: What, to take out the garbage?

RUBY: Yeah.

BIG CED: Uh OK, sure, yeah, it's easier with two anyway.

BIG CED *and* RUBY *go outside and together drag the garbage can from outside the garage to the curb.*

BIG CED: Ruby, you alright?

RUBY: Yeah, I'm OK. I just broke up with Poppo.

BIG CED: You did what?

RUBY: I broke up with Poppo. *(Pause.)* Look, Cedric, I really like you, but I can't wait around forever. So, are you gonna ask me out to a soda at Ralphie's or not?

BIG CED: Ruby, I'ma buy you anything you want at Ralphie's, anything, a slice a' pizza, a burger with super large fries, a corn dog, a—

RUBY: No, I don't want all a' that, Cedric. I just want a soda, a root beer, one root beer and you.

RUBY *and* BIG CED *engage in a passionate kiss.*

BIG CED: I wanna funk with you.

RUBY: I wanna funk with you too.

They kiss again. Enter DP, *peeping his head out just in time to catch* BIG CED *and* RUBY *kissing.*

DP: Dang!

DP *goes back into the garage.*

DP: Ay Ruby and Cedric gettin' it on, man. Poppo, did you know about this?

POPPO: Shut up, DP, I ain't in the mood right now, man.

DP: Oh ay Falcon here too.

Enter FALCON *with* BIG CED, RUBY *behind him.*

DP: Hey what it is, Falcon? How they treatin' you down in Sheffield, man?

FALCON: Oh it's OK. How are you guys doing?

DP: Oh we alright.

RUBY: Fine.

BIG CED: Yeah, we're cool, man, just practicin' and everything.

FALCON: So hey, you guys, I got something to tell you. Um . . . I talked to Boogie Jones last week.

BIG CED: You talked to Boogie Jones?

RUBY: *The* Boogie Jones?

DP: "Stay black Stay black" Boogie Jones?

FALCON: Yeah, that's him.

RUBY: Wait, you mean you actually talked to him?

FALCON: Yeah, he took me to lunch last Saturday, and he . . .

DP: Boogie Jones took you to lunch? Man, what did he order?

POPPO: Who cares what he ordered, DP. I wanna know why he took you to lunch?

DP: Yeah, man, like does he like our sound? Does he dig our style?

FALCON: He said he did.

DP: What? That's it, this is the best day of my life, man, this is it, even better than my ninth birthday party.

POPPO: Yeah, but wait, hold up, why did he go to Falcon, huh? I mean I sing all the lead parts. Shoot, man, Boogie shoulda' came to me, man.

DP: Who cares, man, I just wanna know what happened.

RUBY: Yeah, what did y'all talk about?

BIG CED: Maybe he wants to give us pointers on how we can win at Dee Dee's?

DP: Maybe he wants to help us get a record contract?

RUBY: Maybe he wants to take us on tour?

BIG CED: Yeah, we could be his backup band!

RUBY: So what did he say, Falcon?

DP: Yeah, what did he say?

BIG CED: Man, this could be our big break.

DP: We goin' straight to the top!

BIG CED: But it all depends on what Boogie Jones wants.

BAND: *What does Boogie Jones want?*

Boogie
What ya want
With the five
Fingers of Funk?

Boogie
What ya want
With the five
Fingers of Funk?

Enter BOOGIE JONES.

DP: *Hey look, y'all, it's Boogie Jones!*
BOOGIE JONES: *Everybody please now gather 'round*
The funkiest cat just hit the town
And I got something here to say
The group right here they sure can play
I caught 'em at Dee Dee's just last spring
And just like me they got they own thing
So I'm gonna lend these fingers a hand
'Cause I got big plans for this band say—
BAND: *Boogie*
What ya want
What-does-Boogie-Jones-want?

With the five
Fingers of Funk?
BOOGIE JONES: *Yeah I'm Boogie, Boogie, baby!*
BAND: *Boogie*
What ya want
BOOGIE JONES: *Woooooh-baby!*
BAND: *With the five*
Fingers of Funk?

BOOGIE JONES:	*Stay Black! Stay Black!*
	Now, Ruby girl, if you join with me
	From your Daddy you'll be free
	And no more workin' and all that jive
	Cause, DP man, you're way too live
	And Big Ced ain't no momma's boy
	Now prove yourself under my employ
	And, man, I'll get you a Cadillac
	And you can fly with me and never come back—ay
BAND:	*Boogie you really want*
BOOGIE JONES:	*I do I really I do I—*
BAND:	*The Five Fingers of Funk?*
BOOGIE JONES:	*Sign on my dotted line*
BAND:	*Boogie*
	You really want?
BOOGIE JONES:	*Come with Boogie*
BAND:	*TheFive Fingers of Funk*
BOOGIE JONES:	*As we shake the world's behind—heiiy!*
BAND:	*Boogie what ya want?*
BOOGIE JONES:	*Come on*
BAND:	*Boogie Jones what ya want?*
BOOGIE JONES:	*Come on y'all*
BAND:	*Boogie what ya want?*
BOOGIE JONES:	*Come on*
BAND:	*With the Five Fingers of Funk*
BOOGIE JONES:	*Ow!*
BAND:	*Boogie what ya want?*
BOOGIE JONES:	*You got my number*
BAND:	*Boogie what ya want?*
BOOGIE JONES:	*My private number*
BAND:	*Boogie Jones what ya want?*
BOOGIE JONES:	*Call me y'all, and let's get groovy*

BAND:	*With the Five*
	Fingers . . .
BOOGIE JONES:	*Come with me and you'll go far*
	Turn y'all into shooting stars
	All your issues will dissolve
	With Boogie
	Jones

Exit BOOGIE JONES.

DP: So what does Boogie Jones want man?

BIG CED: Yeah, Falcon, what did he say?

FALCON: Well uh . . . Boogie's starting a record label. And the first act is a new group he's putting together called the Four Cowboys. And he wants me to be in it.

DP: You mean Boogie don't want the Five Fingers of Funk?

BIG CED: He only wants Falcon. He doesn't want us.

FALCON: Yeah, but I told him I wasn't gonna leave you guys or nothin' like that. And he said I can be in both groups if I want to.

DP: Man, this is bullshit, man! Shoot, all this time I thought Boogie Jones was a genius.

POPPO: Boogie Jones is a genius. Say, Falcon, what he say a band should do, you know to get rich and famous and stuff?

FALCON: Well I don't know, but Boogie says he's gonna introduce us to all the record and radio people in the industry.

POPPO: See, marketing, that's what I've been tryna tell y'all this whole time.

BIG CED: Wait, but, Falcon, how you gonn' come all the way from Sheffield and rehearse with two bands, man?

FALCON: No, well, the Four Cowboys rehearse in Sheffield. Boogie Jones, he lives in Sheffield.

DP: Boogie Jones lives in Sheffield? Man, you lyin', man, Boogie live in the ghetto.

FALCON: No, he doesn't, man, I mean I went to his mansion and everything.

POPPO: What his mansion look like, man?

FALCON: Aw it's really nice, he's got like twelve bedrooms, a huge deck, and his swimming pool is shaped like a giant Afro pick, man.

POPPO: An Afro pick–shaped swimming pool? Man, that sounds cool, man. Hey, Falcon, can I join the band too? I mean if you can be in two bands, I can do it too, right? The Four Cowboys, let's make it the Five Cowboys!

FALCON: Well, that would be cool with me, man, but Boogie Jones wants to keep all the band members white and funky.

POPPO: White and funky?

DP: Yeah, Poppo, white and funky. Which means there ain't no room for your black behind in they kind of funk, you dig? But I ain't even worried 'cause check this out—four white boys with a watered-down sound will never groove like us.

BIG CED: Yeah, man, why you wanna join some fake outfit like that when the funk is right here?

FALCON: But, Cedric, I wanna do both. The Four Cowboys is not my idea of real funk, but maybe I can learn something from it, especially being in the studio and working with the equipment, maybe I can get something out of it that can help me, and help us in the future.

BIG CED: Oh so you doin' this for us, huh?

FALCON: No, well, I mean partly, but also this way I can be in Sheffield part of the time. Man, it's hard to make this commute out here, I mean you guys are my friends, but I have some friends out there now, and it's not such a bad place as I thought. You guys should come hang with me at the mall sometime.

DP: The mall? Falcon, what the hell are you talkin' about? Like get your head out the clouds and come down to reality, man. 'Cause the truth is, you can't be funky and unfunky at the same time, man. So you gotta choose, make a choice right now, who you gonn' be, and who you gonn' be with?

FALCON: But why do I have to choose? Huh? Tell me, DP, why do I have to choose? You're just like my Pa, tryna force me into a tiny little box, where my friends can only be this, and my neighbors can only be this, and the kind of music I like can only be this, not that. Well later for that, DP, and later for you, man! I'm tired of being forced to choose one life over the other, man, I don't have to choose.

DP: You already made the choice once you became a Klansman, oh excuse me, a cowboy. And dig it, I ain't gonn' be in a band with nobody that plays both sides of the fence, so now everybody in the band gonna have to choose. See 'cause it's either him or me, you dig? If this white boy stays in the group, then I go. Now what y'all gonn' do?

BIG CED: Wait a minute, DP, I'm not even there yet, man. 'Cause like I'm still tryna understand what's happenin' here. So, Falcon, you gonn' try and be in two bands at the same time? Man, that means you only gonna be here for half the practices, and that's gonn' mess us up, man. I mean like, how can you do this to us, after all this music we've made and everything we've been through? Man, how can you do this to me, man?

FALCON: I'm not doing anything to you, man.

BIG CED: You done changed, Falcon.

DP: And you stealin' from us.

FALCON: What?

DP: You heard me, honkie! You takin' all of our music, all our riffs, all these grooves that we done sweated out through these years, and you gonn give 'em to a white group with a cheesy sound that make even Poppo's songs sound funky.

POPPO: Hey, forget you, DP.

DP: Later, Poppo, OK.

RUBY: Well, hey, look guys, I mean maybe he can do both.

DP: Say what?

BIG CED: What you talkin' 'bout, Ruby?

RUBY: Maybe he can do it all. I mean I live in two worlds, tryna be the deacon's daughter over here, and the keyboardist in the band over here.

BIG CED: Yeah, and it drives you crazy.

RUBY: Yeah, but I still do it. All I'm sayin' is it's doable, Cedric, that's all I'm sayin.

DP: Ruby, you gonn' side with him? This cracker? This honkie?

RUBY: Don't call him names like that, DP!

DP: Shut up, Ruby!

BIG CED: Don't talk to her like that, DP.

DP: I'ma talk how I want, man, shoot, you ain't no boss a' me, and you sure ain't no leader. Maybe if you would a' stepped up and been the leader earlier like you was supposed to, maybe none a' this woulda happened in the first place.

BIG CED: Oh, so now this is my fault now? Falcon joinin' another band, Poppo and all his troubles, us not winnin' at Dee Dee's is all cause a' me?

RUBY: Hey! Everyone be quiet for one second, please. Look, I am so tired of all this macho man bullshit. All of you, posturing with your chests out, I'm so tired of it. And, DP, tell me to shut up again, and watch me slap you into next week.

DP: OK, OK, sorry, just be cool, Ruby, I ain't got no problem with you, it's him *(Pointing to* FALCON.*)* that I'm angry wit'.

FALCON: DP, I'm not a honkie man, and I'm not a cracker, and I'm not The Man. I'm a guitar player, and I like to play music.

BIG CED: Then why can't you play with us?

FALCON: I am!

BIG CED: But you been goin' behind our back talkin' to Boogie Jones about all this, and never tellin' us nothin'?

RUBY: Cedric, he's tellin' us right now. What is wrong with you all, I don't see what the problem is?

BIG CED: Well you must be blind then, Ruby. 'Cause how's he gonna travel all this way every day and rehearse with us and with them. It's too much.

RUBY: Cedric, why don't you let Falcon decide what is and isn't too much.

BIG CED: Ruby, why you doin' this?

RUBY: Doin' what?

BIG CED: Falcon's tryna break up the band, and you helpin' him
do it.

RUBY: Cedric, what are you . . .

BIG CED: Where's your loyalty, Ruby? Huh? Or do you have
something you need to tell me?

RUBY: Tell you?

BIG CED: I seen the way you be lookin' at Falcon, I've been checkin'
you out for a long time now. You, you wanna be with him, don't
cha? You don't wanna be with me, you wanna be with him. You
think he's cute, and he's got everything goin' for him, don't he?

RUBY: Cedric, what are you saying?

BIG CED: Don't lie to me Ruby! *(Pause.)* See, I knew it, I knew if I
went steady with you, you would cheat on me and go behind my
back. My momma was right. *(Pause.)*

RUBY: OK, you got me, Cedric. I do like Falcon. Me and him been
seeing each other for six months, ain't that right, Falcon?

FALCON: Uh . . .

RUBY: Come here, baby.

RUBY *grabs* FALCON's *head and forcefully kisses him.* FALCON *stands
there confused.*

RUBY: You found me out, Cedric. You and I. It's over.

Exit RUBY.

BIG CED: Wait, Ruby, I'm sorry, I . . .

FALCON: Cedric, man, I don't know what that was about.

BIG CED: Get out, Falcon.

FALCON: But Cedric . . .

BIG CED: Get out, man! I want you out of my garage. Yeah, go join
your white friends in Sheffield.

DP: Yeah, man, go join them white boys in Sheffield.

BIG CED: And don't you ever come back here neither. You ain't
welcomed here no more.

FALCON: OK, OK, if that's how you guys want it.

POPPO: I still wouldn't mind goin' with you, man. Say, talk to Boogie Jones, and see if he maybe couldn't . . .

FALCON *unplugs his guitar and exits.*

DP: Man, I'm outta here, man.

BIG CED: Wait, where you goin'?

DP: Man, I gotta find a job, man. And ain't nothin' goin' on around here, so, hey later, y'all.

BIG CED: Wait, wait, DP, are we still a band? DP?

DP *exits, leaving* BIG CED *and* POPPO *alone. There's a long, awkward pause before either of them speak.*

BIG CED: So, what are we gonna do?

POPPO: About what?

BIG CED: About the band?

POPPO: Huh nothin', man. The band is finished.

BIG CED: Naw, naw, man, we can't be finished, we just can't be.

POPPO: It's over, Big Ced, finito, end of story.

BIG CED: Naw, I can't believe that, Poppo . . .

> *I can't believe there won't be another song*
> *To sing—baby*
> *Can't accept the fact that what we had*
> *Has gone*
> *Permanently*

Lights up on DP *inside a fast-food restaurant.*

DP:
> *Good evening, sir*
> *Are you taking applications?*

Lights on FALCON *at a bus stop.*

| FALCON: | *Where is the 7:15?* |
| | *To scoop me far away* |

Lights up on RUBY *alone in her daddy's church.*

RUBY:	*I was so in love I thought I knew*
	My constitution—baby!
	Then they had to drag a sista' through
	All of
	Their issues
BAND:	*Forget those fools*
RUBY:	*Who needs 'em?*
BAND:	*Later for those dudes*
RUBY:	*I don't need 'em*
BAND:	*I'll be just fine, out here on my own*
POPPO:	*And now it's over*
	This whole relationship is over
	And, man, it's drivin' me so crazy
	'Cause this band it was my baby
	And now she left me
BIG CED:	*I know it's all my fault*
POPPO:	*I broke up the band*
FALCON:	*If I hadn't joined the Cowboys*
RUBY:	*If I didn't go with Poppo and Cedric*
DP:	*If I didn't call Falcon a honkie and told 'im to split*
POPPO:	*If I had been on time all this time*
BIG CED:	*If I had faith in the grooves that were mine*
BAND:	*If I had funk!*
	Take it back take it back
	All them things ya said to me
	We nev-er will be
	Later for y'all
	Later for y'all—yeah
	I'm so glad it's senior year

Soon
You
I won't
See

Wastin' my time
Wastin' my time
Playin' in that little garage

You
Never
Could
Keep a groove

Thank you God
Thank you god
'Cause I don't have to go back there

Surely
This is the end

RUBY: *But what am I to do now that it's gone*
The funk
No more!
Guess I'll play the organ for the church choir
Daddy will be so pleased

DP: *Why do I want this job?*
Um, my goal in life is to dip corn
Dogs

FALCON: *Boogie Jones says we*
Should dye our hair
Blond so we
Can appear
White . . .
As can be
Is this the real me?

BAND: *This is the real thing*

POPPO: *'Cause now it's over*

BAND:

> This whole relationship is over
> And, man, it's drivin' me so crazy
> 'Cause this band it was my baby
> But—now, the dream's gone
> I better get somethin' to fall back on
> And all my friends I know they hate me
> But my love was never maybe
>
> I guess this is just reality
> The way things they really supposed be
> When you grow you know it's fantasy
> All the dreams that floated in your brain
> So now you drink your mornin' coffee
> Hopin' it will help ya stay awake
> 'Cause your life is so borin'
> And you'll never be funky

Exit RUBY, FALCON, *and* DP.

BIG CED: Poppo, you gotta do somethin'. Fix this, man, make it right, do somethin'! See, 'cause I don't care what DP say, I've seen us get better, and we wouldn't be as good as we are if it wasn't for your hard work, all the promotions, the flyer designs, all the hustlin' you did for us gettin' us all those shows. Man, Dee Dee wouldn't even know our name if it wasn't for you. Man, you are the leader of this band. So now do somethin', man!

POPPO: But I'm outta ideas, Big Ced. There's nothin' I can do. Plus I got bigger problems.

BIG CED: Bigger problems? Like what? Like what, Poppo?

POPPO: Man, look, you don't understand, 'cause, see, you got everything, Ced. I mean, I wish I could just trade places with you. I would be so happy—

BIG CED: Poppo, I'm two hundred and fifty pounds, and you look like a model in Ebony. So why would you ever wanna trade places with me?

POPPO: Because you got it all, man. A loving momma, a musical talent for song writin', and now Ruby.

BIG CED: Ay I wanna talk to you about that.

POPPO: You ain't gotta say nothin', man. It was obvious to all of us from day one that you two dug each other. I'm just sorry I got in the way, makin' it all difficult. I guess if I had a talent it would be that. Makin' any situation I enter into that much more difficult. Anyway I better split. I'll see you around, Big Ced.

POPPO *makes a move to leave, then turns back around toward* BIG CED.

POPPO: One thing I never understood, man. Through all these years I've dogged you out, callin' you names, not lettin' us do your songs, takin' the girl you liked. But still with all that, you always looked out for me, man, why?

BIG CED: Why? Because, man, you're my brother, that's why. I mean, didn't you look out for me, for us, in your own way?

POPPO: I—I don't know. I guess so.

BIG CED: OK well, there ya go.

POPPO: Yeah. Alright well, I'll catch ya later, Big Ced.

BIG CED: Tomorrow.

POPPO: Yeah, tomorrow.

Exit POPPO. *Alone,* BIG CED *looks around the now empty garage space. Enter* BIG CED'S MOMMA.

BIG CED'S MOMMA: Cedric! Dinner's ready.

BIG CED: I'm commin', Momma. Let me just switch off the amps.

BIG CED'S MOMMA: OK, baby.

SLIM *walks up behind* POPPO. *Exit* BIG CED, RUBY, DP, *and* FALCON.

SLIM: Hey young blood.

POPPO: Ay Slim. I know I messed up. I still got some of the money, man, and I'll try to get the rest . . .

SLIM: It's OK, Poppo. Take what you got and put it in this bag for me.

POPPO: Alright. Are you still my best friend?

SLIM: Always, young blood. Put it in the bag, Poppo.

SLIM *hands* POPPO *a green duffel bag. As* POPPO *puts the money into the bag,* SLIM *pulls out a long, silver gun.*

POPPO: Slim, are you my daddy?

SLIM *shoots* POPPO *in the head. Enter* BIG CED *out of breath.*

BIG CED: Poppo!

Startled, SLIM *reacts, shooting* BIG CED *in the stomach. He collapses to the ground. Hear* BIG CED'S MOMMA *scream. Exit* SLIM. *Church bells ring. Scene moves to a funeral. Dressed in black,* RUBY, DP, *and* FALCON *play a gospel-tinged version of the classic song "You'll Never Walk Alone."* RUBY *sings lead.*

RUBY:
When you walk through the storm
Hold your head up high
And don't be afraid of the dark
At the end of the storm
Is a golden sky
And the sweet silver song of a lark

Walk on through the wind
Walk on through the rain
Tho' your dreams be tossed and blown
Walk on, walk on
With hope in your heart
And you'll never walk alone
You'll never walk alone

Song ends. Scene shifts back to the garage. POPPO*'s funeral has just ended.* RUBY, FALCON, DP, *and* BIG CED *enter into the garage and stay silent for a moment or two.* BIG CED *moves slowly in pain. For several seconds, no one in the band says anything.*

DP: Man, Poppo . . . Damn!

DP *loses his cool and begins to knock over his drum set. The others try to calm him down.*

BIG CED: Be cool, DP, that ain't gonn' bring 'im back.

DP: I know but it's messed up. See, this is how they get you, you dig? This is how The Man work, and he's conspirin' against all of us.

BIG CED: DP . . .

DP: The Man did it again, took another brother from us. Man, how long is this gonna happen before we say that we ain't takin' it no more! Well I ain't takin' it no more, ya understand? We can't do this no m—

BIG CED: DP! Shut the hell up, I don't wanna hear another word about The Man. The Man is us. You, me, we in control. What we need to do is practice and keep practicin', and I guarantee you, we gonn' win this Friday at Dee Dee's. Now, are y'all ready to go higher?

DP: We ready.

RUBY: Yeah, let's do it.

FALCON: All the way, man.

BIG CED *picks up his bass ready to play. Enter* BIG CED'S MOMMA *at the top of the stairs.*

BIG CED'S MOMMA: Cedric, it's time to eat.

BIG CED: I can't right now, momma.

BIG CED'S MOMMA *comes down the stairs.*

BIG CED'S MOMMA: Cedric, it's dinnertime!

BIG CED: I'm not hungry. And we gotta practice, momma.

BIG CED'S MOMMA: Uh uh, practice is over. And your friends can leave before they get you killed.

BIG CED *looks around the room at* DP, RUBY, *and* FALCON. *He then turns back and faces his mother.*

BIG CED: I can't eat just 'cause you need me to. I can't live at your table. I'm a bass player, but I'm not daddy. I gotta play my own song.

BIG CED *turns away from his mother and addresses the band.*

BIG CED: Alright, let's get into it. Let's get . . . funky. One, two, three, and . . .

Enter DR. FUNK. *Lights out on the band.*

DR. FUNK: Five Fingers of Funk
                     Went on to win at Dee Dee's
                     And soon the world moved to their beat
                     And the funk, it lived on
                     Because the funk cannot die
                     From my eight-track to your iPod
                     Through time this groove has made heads nod
                     Even today
                     In the year 2008
                     You can't go no place without hearin' . . . the
                     funk!

As FIVE FINGERS OF FUNK *continues to play, enter radio DJ 1, 2 and 3.*

DJ 3: Hey y'all, WKISS kiss FM, this is the new one from 50 cent, and he uses that old groove from Five Fingers of Funk, oh, I love this one!

DJ 1: Hey, Mr. Majestic on your radio, here's the latest from Young Jeezy, check out how he rhymes over this old record by, who is this? Hmm, some group called Five Fingers of Funk.

DJ 3: Here's the new one from Beyoncé, she call this "The Shake Attack," and she sound good too, y'all, especially with that sample she got from Five Fingers of Funk.

DJ 2: WBKS 106.5 on your dial, this is the sister girl call Uw Child, and I got the new one from Five Fingers of Funk.

DJ 1: WPOOK—we pook commin' at ya with the Old School Hour from twelve to one, now it's time to have some fun, so let's get groovy, y'all, with Five Fingers of Funk!

Lights up on, BIG CED, DP, RUBY, *and* FALCON. *They're a few years older, at the height of their careers, playing to an arena filled with fans. They launch into a super-charged version of their theme song, "Five Fingers of Funk."*

BIG CED:	*Through these times*
	We've come a long ways since the days of
	Groovin' in my momma's garage
	Back then we thought it'd be so easy
	To achieve everything just
	Switch on the amp and be a star
RUBY:	*But with pain round every corner*
	Hearts that shook with coldness
BIG CED AND RUBY:	*Never thought we'd make it this far*
BIG CED:	*We even lost our brother long the way*
	And though you count four on the stage
	Let us tell y'all who we are
	We are the grooviest band that you know
BAND:	*This funk is twenty times better than dope*
	If you ain't know before, well, now you know
BIG CED:	*Slap me five, y'all!*
BAND:	*Five Fingers of Funk*
	Five Fingers of Funk

Five Fingers of Funk
Five Fingers of Funk

Five Fingers of Funk
Five Fingers of Funk
Five Fingers of Funk
Five Fingers of Funk
Five Fingers of Funk
Five Fingers of Funk

END

PROM

Conceived by Whit MacLaughlin

Developed by Children's Theatre Company and
New Paradise Laboratories

The world premier of *Prom* was directed by Whit MacLaughlin and
opened on March 5, 2004, at Franklin Art Works, Minneapolis.
The script for the 2005–6 season, reproduced here, was debuted
on the Children's Theatre Company stage. *Prom* was coproduced
by Children's Theatre Company and New Paradise Laboratories
and was funded in part by The Wallace Foundation Leadership
and Excellence in Arts Participation initiative and the Multi-
Arts Production Fund of the Creative Capital Foundation and the
Rockefeller Foundation.

CREATIVE TEAM
Scenic design: Matt Saunders
Costume design: Rosemarie E. McKelvey
Lighting design: Rebecca Fuller
Sound design: Whit MacLaughlin
Production supervisor: Rebecca Brown
Assistant director: Lee Ann Etzold
Stage manager: Erin Tatge
Assistant stage manager: Danae Schniepp

CAST

RILEY CONNORS	David Belt
BROOKE BYRON	Laine Buntrock
RIKKI MCHERRING	Rachel Ihrig Cooper
LEAH GINSBERG	Eva "Chava" Curland
CHRISTIAN DUCOMB	Curtis Fox
LENI "MAGGIE MAY" STONE	Nadia Hulett
JAZZLYN RODRIGUEZ	Jennifer Lagos

CORNELIUS "NEIL" WELCH III	Theo Langason
JOEL DUNCAN	Eric Mayson
GRETCHEN EUN AE	Joann Oudekerk
VIKTOR E. FAWKES	Kyle Roman
TRACY ZEMKE	Casey Smart
MILO MIELKE (Principal)	Gerald Drake
TANIA CHARITY-SCARBOROUGH (Guidance Counselor)	Marvette Knight
SYLVIA SWANSON (Drama Teacher)	Laura A. Osnes
CARSON WATCHKE (Chemistry Teacher)	Dan Selon
PAULETTE SELKE (French Teacher)	Autumn Ness
RICH E. DECKER (Assistant Principal)	Samuel G. Roberson Jr.
DON HJELLE (Medieval History Teacher)	Reed Sigmund
REFEREE	Chris Carlson

PRE-SHOW

In the lobby, two of the male students are playing a song. A simple set-up—guitar, bass, amp. As the audience enters, they sing the song and speak the dialogue in a continuous loop until the performance begins.

> *Name is Ryan,*
> *And I've been eyeing,*
> *This girl for a couple of years.*
> *But I don't think she know that I exist.*
> *I think I'll ask her to the Prom,*
> *you know it can't go wrong,*
> *cause it's me, right?*
>
> *My name is Ryan,*
> *And I've been trying*
> *To write a poem to ask a*
> *Girl to the dance with me.*
> *If she said yes,*
> *I must confess*

> *My life would be a success*
> *What would I say to make her mine*
> *It seems I've tried a thousand times,*
> *To ask her if she'll be mine . . .*
> *(Spoken.)* Here she comes.

JOEL DUNCAN: Umm, hello.

RILEY CONNORS: Hi.

JOEL: Ummm, well you think you'd ever go?

RILEY: Go where?

JOEL: Actually I have a poem for you, Roses are red, violets are blue,
   I want to go to the Prom with you.

RILEY: NO!!

> *My name is Ryan*
> *And now I'm crying*
> *Because the poem I spilled my soul in was spit in my*
>   *face.*
> *I have an idea!*
> *I'll take a thousand candles*
> *And put 'em on her front lawn*
> *Spelling out a question mark*
> *Along with the word "Prom"*

The Next Day

JOEL: Umm hello.

RILEY: Hello again.

JOEL: So will you go?

RILEY: Go where?

JOEL: Didn't you get my message?

RILEY: What message?

JOEL: The candles, in your yard . . .

RILEY: That was you?

JOEL: Yeah . . .

RILEY: THAT WAS YOU?

JOEL: Yeah . . .

RILEY: IT BURNED DOWN MY HOUSE!!!!!!!

> My name is Ryan
> And now I'm dying
> I was forced to go to the Prom with my mom.
> "Come on sweetie, let's walk down the red carpet,
> You gonna give me a kiss? Ha ha ha ha ha."
> Here she comes,
> Oh to hell with the plan,
> I'm going to be her man.
> I'll kiss her on the lips.
> And she'll know what she has missed.
> The time is now,
> Don't be a coward,
> We'll have a hundred babies,
> And name one Howard.
>
> His name is Bryan,
> Turns out she was lying,
> He was the champion of the Fair Oaks Boxing Team.
> I guess we were never meant to be together, oh well.
> There's always next year!

THE SET

At center is a wrestling mat, the white ring prominently outlined. Above it, the same diameter as the white ring, floats a halolike chandelier of electric lights. A metal frame, like a pyramid, surrounds the wrestling mat. It is strung with yellow caution tape. On either side of the wrestling mat is artificial turf marked with football yardage lines. At either end of the artificial turf are tackling mats. Printed on the mat at one end is: PAST. Printed on the mat at the other end is: FUTURE. On the stage wall above the PAST mat is a projection screen. Off to either side, a table with a punch bowl and plastic cups, and two chalkboards on wheels. Helium-filled weather balloons hang at the edges of the playing space.

As the audience enters, the chaperones are onstage, wandering, waiting. They stay in the shadows, outside the center white wrestling ring. Each of the following monologues is heard in voice-over. As each chaperone's voice-over begins, they move into the white ring and perform a dance/series of abstract gestures. Behind them, on the projection screen, high school photos of them are projected.

TANIA: I'm Tania Charity-Scarborough, Fair Oaks High School Guidance Counselor. When I was in high school, I was class president. But I was socially awkward. I had a white boyfriend at the time. But everyone thought I should be dating the captain of the basketball team, who was black. They elected me prom princess. I got the Chicano and Black vote and just squeaked it out. The point is, I liked the margins between things. We ended up dancing in the waves down an empty beach at the margin between night and day just as the tide was coming in.

CARSON: My name is Carson Watchke. I teach chemistry. I went to the prom with Amanda Jeffries. I thought maybe she was a lesbian. Nope. In actuality she wasn't, she had this boyfriend and . . . well . . .

I rented a costume instead of a tux: a purple suit with pink ruffles and a purple eighties rock mullet. We looked so great everyone cheered. After the dance we rode on a roller coaster way too many times. I idled the car at an intersection while she threw up over and over and over again onto the dark road.

RICH: Rich Decker, Assistant Principal. I didn't exactly date in high school—I had what you might call "associates." Movies, talk, dinner . . . some making out. Nothing serious. When the prom came around, I wanted to take someone special, but there was no one who seemed just right. So, I took the best date ever—which was no date. At dinner, I left a space at the table. And at the prom I danced like crazy. We took a picture—I put my arm around thin air. I didn't have to pay too much attention to *anybody*. It was great.

SYLVIA: My name is Sylvia Swanson and I teach English and drama. My prom was so happy. Peter made me feel like a princess . . . like, I didn't know anyone . . . Pete introduced me to all his friends . . .

We danced . . . every song was about us . . . we jumped puddles in the rain . . . great, corny stuff like that . . .

Then came the smooch. That was like icing on a cookie. We wound up dating all through college. *(Pause.)* Now it all feels a little strange. I keep wondering: do I miss him enough?

DON: Bye! Bye! Bye, Mom! Bye, Dad! Don Hjelle, Medieval History. The prom was my first date ever. I drove to Jackie's house feeling sick. For some reason she had refused to talk to me for the past two weeks. I pulled up to her house in my sister's Bronco II. Not the best car, but my car had broken down. I was insanely nervous. I approached the door with her corsage.

Hi.

She stormed toward me, screamed "no f-ing flowers," then, she threw them on the ground and stomped on them.

I could tell myself that I was scarred forever, but, actually, I think I'm pretty happy now.

PAULETTE: I'm Miss Paulette Selke. I'm the French teacher. Typically, there were five couples up for prom coronation—four obvious popular couples and one reject couple. I was paired that year with the biggest loser in the school, JP Tanner—all he ever did was talk about real estate—so I doubt that we were one of the popular couples. They made you pair up and walk in two-by-two. At the last moment I told him to jump on my back—he was really small—and I carried him out there piggyback while they did the crown over the head thing.

MILO *looks through his binoculars.*

UBER VOICE *(female, dispassionate. Heard in voice-over.)*: The PROM: a keyhole that we pass through on our way to our own set of keys.

RICH *enters, jingling keys. He locks the "FUTURE" door and goes to the cafeteria.*

RICH: There better not be anybody in there! *(Authoritatively, official.)* Can I have your attention, please? Can I have your attention, please? A couple of announcements about the exits. Exit is spelled E X I T—Exit. Exit. If you look around you and can read, you will find all of the exits out of this zone. In case of emergency please read the sign first before helping those who can't. Also, in an emergency, please refrain from running into this wall or crashing out those windows, creating another emergency, which we won't have time to address. *(Pointing to the FUTURE.)* That exit there, well, that exit is a little strange. I have a prepared statement from the Principal Milo M. Mielke. *(Reading.)* "When you walked in, that exit was an entrance; when you walk out, that entrance will have become an exit. You entered from the present, and you will exit into the future." *(Slight pause.)* What that means, I don't know. *(Smiling again.)* Keep it real.

RICH *exits through the dressing rooms.*

UBER VOICE: The PROM: there is only one exit and that exit is the future.

CARSON *prepares to mop the mat.*

UBER VOICE: Chaperone: An older person who attends and supervises a social gathering for young people.

CARSON *mops the mat.*

UBER VOICE: Chaperone: A guide or companion whose purpose is to restrict activity and ensure politeness.

PAULETTE (*through a megaphone*): Everyone, everyone, attention, écoutez, écoutez, eeoo, eeoo. J'espere que tout le monde ça va bien. Je suis le professeur de français, Paulette Selke. Je suis trés heureuse (*Smile.*), et je suis trés nerveuse, parce que; quelle heure est-il? Quelle heure? Il est huit heures, on ve commence la *grand march* dans trois minute—un, deux, trois. Woo woo woo woo! Il est necessaire que pour vous dit, "Je danse!! Je mange!! Je reçois un biss." (*Kiss.*) AAAAH? Bon! Merci.

The doors at the back of the stage fly open. Teens tear into the room, cheering, running, hollering, preparing for the grand march. They fill the playing space.

TANIA: Ladies and gentlemen, kids, kids, kids, harness, channel, ascend, converge, redirect, release. Could we please take your places for the Grand March—yes, yes, breathe, breathe . . .
UBER VOICE: At the PROM, the future gets rehearsed.
DON: Well, everybody looks great. Hi. Hello everyone. OK, well I think we're ready to get marching here, huh Paulette?

The students line up at the far end of the artificial turf in front of the PAST mat. PAULETTE and DON stand at a microphone off to the side of the white ring and announce each student. As their names are called, the students process to the center of the white ring.

PAULETTE: Oui means yes. First off, here comes Leah Ginsburg. (*Applause.*) Leah likes romance, flower chains, and beatnik poetry (*Snapping fingers.*). Can you dig it?
DON: I can dig it.
PAULETTE: I knew you could. Leah's pet peeve is people who belong to school clubs, and she secretly feels small. I think that's because she is so short and cute, cute, cute. (*Applause.*)
DON: OK, step up to the plate, Mr. Riley Connors. (*Applause.*) This young man is a big fan of poetry, small tattoos, and one-on-one talks. While touring the region with his band, he is likely to

avoid bullies, politics, small spaces, and bees. He sleeps with a night light and knows how to ballroom dance. *(Applause.)*

CARSON: Smile! *(Leah poses, Carson snaps her photo.)*

PAULETTE: Coming your way is Jazzlyn Rodriguez. *(Applause.)* Jazzlyn is obsessed with ballet, learning about different cultures, and Dino's gyros. I know someone else who likes Dino's gyros.

DON: I like the chicken.

PAULETTE: Her favorite subject is French, and I'm crossing my fingers that she can save enough to come on the French trip this summer ee ee ee. *(Cut the can-can.)* And it's important to note, she has a boyfriend who's older, but she will flirt with *anyone* because she's that secure in her relationship. Thank you, Jazzy. *(Applause.)*

CARSON: Smile! *(Jazzlyn poses. Carson snaps her photo.)*

PAULETTE: Our next marcher is Gretchen Eun Ae—*(Applause.)* Gretchen is a senior who likes graffiti, piercings, boys, *and* girls—oh, I guess that's everybody. She is good at darts and recently ran away from home. I have a feeling one was the cause of the other. Gretchen! *(Applause.)*

DON: All right, next up is her date, Mr. Viktor Estoban Fawkes. *(Applause.)* I didn't know your middle name was Estoban. Wait. Your middle initial is E? Viktor *E.* Fawkes. Viktor E Fawkes. Victory Fawkes . . . wow. That's awesome. Anyway, uh, Viktor likes logic and is a member of the chess club. Although he is, in his own words, ferociously charismatic, he has no steady girlfriend. And just in case you were wondering, his dad makes robots. *(Applause.)*

CARSON: Smile! *(Gretchen and Viktor pose. Carson snaps their photo.)*

PAULETTE: Our next student is Tracy Zemke—*(Applause.)* Tracy likes parties and skirts. She dislikes Spanish class, sticky tables, and loud nose breathing. When she's not at home watching Lifetime, you might find her dancing, applying eyeliner, or lying. *(Applause.)* And she's here tonight with . . . who's her date?

DON: Christian.

PAULETTE: She's here with Christian? Holy crap!

DON: Yeah, this is awkward. OK, here he is, the sluttiest man in school, Mr. Christian Ducomb. *(Applause.)* This talented quarterback only plays football because his dad makes him. Socially insecure, Christian fears freezing to death and is secretly in love with fellow classmate Joel, but not in a sexual way.

CHRISTIAN: Hey, Brooke! Check this out! *(Kisses TRACY.)*

DON: This is really awkward. He likes pretty people and Diesel jeans, but hates nerds, party poopers, and conservatives. *(Applause.)*

CARSON: Smile! *(TRACY and CHRISTIAN pose. CARSON snaps their photo.)*

DON: Next up is little miss dance team and Christian's *former* girlfriend, Brooke Byron. *(Applause.)* B.B., who incidentally hates to be called B.B., is into traveling and is a member of the Pilates Club. An honor student who wants to shoot for the moon, B.B. spends her free time reading, studying French, and plotting her future. Plus, she's terrified of sex! *(Silence.)* *(Quietly to PAULETTE.)* That's what it says here.

Hey, there's her escort Cornelius Welch III. *(Applause.)* Most people call him Neil. He likes women. He really likes women. He loves women. But he hates milk. This dancing, rapping, beat boxing giant is graduating with a 4.0 and will head to the University of Pennsylvania this fall. He would prefer that you didn't know that he gets frustrated, even teary-eyed if his clothes don't match. Ladies and gentlemen, my buddy, Cornelius Welch III. *(Applause.)*

CARSON: Smile! *(BROOKE poses. CARSON snaps her photo.)*

PAULETTE: And next, we have Hurricane Katrina-I-mean-Rikki McHerring. *(Applause.)* In her busy schedule of truancy and stealing from American Eagle, Rikki finds time to enjoy makeover shows, and letting people smoke in her car. She dislikes scrunchies, dreadlocks, and hot freshman girls. Rikki is going stag this year. After being ditched at the last prom, we sure hope this one goes better. And Rikki, if it doesn't, my door is always open. Until 3:30. Rikki! *(Applause.)*

CARSON: Smile! (RIKKI *poses.* CARSON *snaps her photo.*)

DON: The last fella to ease on down the road is Mr. Joel Duncan. (*Applause.*) Joel wears thick glasses. This busy brunette loves thinking, writing music, and politics. He is senior class president and the only male in the Knitting Club. That's true, last year for my birthday he made me a really beautiful scarf. Thanks for that, by the way. Congratulations, Joel, your classmates voted you "most likely to stand on a street corner, make a speech, and spend a night in county lockup." (*Applause.*)

PAULETTE: And finally, he's here tonight with his BFF—Best Friend Forever Leni Stone! (*Applause.*) Leni is a boy's name, but she is a girl—so respect it. BFF Girl Leni likes eyes, smiles, and the idea of peace. She dislikes Starbucks and celebrities and has a phobia of rejection, suffocation, and being broke her whole life. She enjoys writing class and wants to travel the world and join the Peace Corps. (*Applause.*)

CARSON: Smile! (JOEL *and* LENI *pose.* CARSON *snaps their photo*)

PAULETTE: Ladies and gentlemen, this concludes our 2006 Fair Oaks High Grand March. Give yourselves a hand!

MILO (*taking his place in the center ring*): Welcome, welcome, welcome. I, your principal, Mr. Milo M. Mielke, on behalf of the entire staff of Fair Oaks High welcome you. Welcome. Welcome. Welcome. Illumination through books. Prom is a four-letter word. And like tape or zoom or face or pain or love, what ultimately matters is what we do with it. (*Spotlights.*) Tradition is to humans what instinct is to animals. Imagine the chaos if animals lost their instincts. So would it be if human beings lost all their traditions. (*Spotlights.*) This year's theme, "Lost in Enchantment," reminds me of my desire to travel. It began with that great American poet Mr. Autry, who said, and I quote, "Home, home on the range where the deer and the antelope play. Where seldom is heard a discouraging word and the skies are not cloudy all day." Remember: Be prepared.

TANIA:	Hut!
	Hut!
	Hut!
CHAPERONES:	Hut!

The CHAPERONES *move into formation on the artificial turf behind* MILO.
A highly choreographed cheer.

CHAPERONES:	You are uniquely you
	How funky is your chicken?
	One man's hat is another man's shoe
	Ripe for the pickin'
	If you can see it you can do it

The chaperones are reluctant to let their students find the future in *Prom* (2006). *Left to right:* Marvette Knight, Reed Sigmund, Autumn Ness, Gerald Drake, Dan Selon, Samuel G. Roberson Jr., and Laura A. Osnes. Photograph by Rob Levine.

But you gotta get on up and get down to it
Heal the world
We are the world
huh, huh, huh, huh
Feel the burn
Peace on earth
Seize the day
Dive in!

MILO: Learning happens.

UBER VOICE: At the PROM you experience the last party of your childhood.

MILO: Here we stand on the precipice of life. Behind us is the past. In front of us and beyond—the future. But tonight, there is only the present. Ms. Charity—

TANIA (*taking her place beside Milo in the center ring*): No moshing. Students: What?!

TANIA: No moshing, no huffing, no lap dances, no tap dances, no hat dances, no heads below the waist, no waists below the buttocks, no punch-drunk love, no lingerie out, no lingerie in, no stink bombs, no cell calls, no sequins, no exit, no refunds, no heckling, no slap happy, no tap happy, no twerking, no simbas, no limbas, no tubas, no zubas, and most importantly of all, no foobahs. Higher plane—higher plane existence.

MILO: Kids, have a real good time. (*Applause.*)

CHAPERONES: Be prepared
                Be prepared
                Be prepared

The REFEREE *enters from the dressing rooms and runs around the room preparing for the prom. He slaps the mat and checks with* MIELKE.

REFEREE: The clock is running. Let's do this thing. (*Blows whistle.*)

UBER VOICE: Fast Dance Number One.

PAULETTE: (*Horn.*)

Entrance of teens around the dance floor. Several teens consider dancing. RIKKI, JAZZLYN, *and* BROOKE *dance.* CHRISTIAN *joins them. The girls leave.* JOEL *and* LENI, *then several more dance.* RILEY *gets carried away.*

REFEREE: *(Whistle then a series of referee semaphore gestures)*
(To RILEY.*)* Hey! *(To crowd.)* Premature choreographic exuber-ance with excessive hip-hop affectation. Busting a move when the night is still young. Penalty: five seconds in the hot box. Ready? *(All stare at* RILEY.*)* *(Whistle.)* Five, four, three, two, let it burn, son . . . *(Pause.)* One. *(Whistle.)*

DON *and* SYLVIA *enter with a chalkboard.* CARSON *and* PAULETTE *enter with another.* CARSON *and* DON *draw arrows mapping out the penalty.* RICH *enters.*

RICH: All right, let's take a look at what went wrong here. We can see here Connors initiates his move way too early. Now I know this kind of "premature action" is common among high school boys, but I *didn't* see it coming from Riley "Boogey Down" Connors. Now let's look at that move in slo-mo and see if we can elucidate where he went wrong. Here—now if Connors had stuck to the classic "step-touch" move or even a simple but edgier "cabbage patch," this entire moment could have played out to a much less embarrassing end. Boogey Down, what happened out there?
RILEY: I guess I just wanted to set the tone.
RICH: Nice hustle, kid.

DON *and* CARSON *strike the chalkboards.*

UBER VOICE: Chaperone: An older person who attends and supervises a social gathering for young people.

LEAH, GRETCHEN, BROOKE, *and* LENI *comfort* RILEY *while the rest look on.*

UBER VOICE: Fast Dance Number Two.
PAULETTE: (Horn.)

CHRISTIAN *asks* BROOKE *to dance.*

UBER VOICE: Slow Dance Number One.
PAULETTE: (Horn.)
Abruptly, a slow dance plays. CHRISTIAN *and* BROOKE *dance. All gaze and gossip.* NEIL *crosses the mat.*

UBER VOICE: Fast Dance Number Three.
PAULETTE: (Horn.)
STUDENTS: Woohooo!!!

Just as abruptly, the music changes again. Dancing. The ring lowers and raises. NEIL *gets carried away.*

REFEREE: (Whistle.) (The REF pulls JAZZLYN away from NEIL.)
    (To BROOKE.) Ma'am. (To NEIL.) What is that? (Semaphoric
    gestures, then to crowd.) Personal foul—Improper use of the
    hands: Intentional Foobah. Penalty: Eight seconds in the hot
    box. Ready? (Whistle.) (All stare at Neil.) Eight, seven, six, five,
    four, three, two, one. (Whistle.)

DON *and* CARSON *enter with chalkboards and draw stick figures depicting the penalty.* RICH *enters slowly.*

RICH: Oh, Mr. Cornelius. Right in front of grandma?

DON *and* CARSON *strike the chalkboards.*

UBER VOICE: At the PROM, the future gets rehearsed.
DON: They're going to go—they're going to run for it—they're gonna
    go—here they come!

VIKTOR, RIKKI, RILEY, *and* JAZZLYN *break for the FUTURE.* TANIA, DON, PAULETTE, *and* RICH *stop them.*

> *They make a second attempt. They are thoroughly rousted.*
> REFEREE *confirms the outcome.*

REFEREE: *(Whistle.)* Students' spontaneous break for the future is no good. There is no score on the play. The clock is still running. Keep on moving. Don't stop groovin'. *(Whistle.)*

LENI: Hey! Look at me!

STUDENTS: I'm an apple!
Let us make our play
Cause you're a little old to stand in the way
Listen up—we know what we need
Give us the keys
and let us proceed
Out!
of!
the way!
The past is in your heads
The future's in our hands
What part of out of the way
Do you not understand?
Huh!

MILO: Ladies and gentlemen. The night is young. *(Rich rattles the keys.)* There is plenty of time ahead. Believe me, you will look back on this as . . . *(Laughs.)* Don't turn your back on what is right in front of you. Enjoy this moment.

UBER VOICE: Fast Dances Numbers Four through Nine.

PAULETTE: *(Horn.)*

STUDENTS *approach the dance floor.*

PAULETTE: *(Horn.)*

STUDENTS *dance in a trance. Halo lowers.*

UBER VOICE *(during the lowering of halo):* At the PROM—everyone is filled with unfulfilled desires. At the PROM—you are on a treasure hunt and you may not believe that the treasure exists. At the PROM—you experience the last party of your childhood.

The students of Fair Oaks High are ready to party. *In no certain order:* Casey Smart, Joann Oudekerk, Kyle Roman, Eric Mayson, Theo Langason, Jennifer Lagos, Nadia Hulett, Curtis Fox, Eva "Chava" Curland, Rachel Ihrig Cooper, Laine Buntrock, and David Belt. Photograph by Rob Levine.

Horn. STUDENTS *kneel.* CARSON *is revealed in the midst of them, dressed in a lab coat and safety goggles. He holds a beaker high in the air, then passes it between the legs of* NEIL *and then* BROOKE. *He drinks from the beaker and howls.*

REFEREE: *(Whistle.)* Students endure nostalgic scrutiny and evaluation. No point on the play. The score: Chaperones o, Students o. Halftime. Punchbowl.

STUDENTS *head for the punch bowl with defiant yelps at the* CHAPERONES. *The* CHAPERONES *dish it right back. Halo raises.*

TANIA: Ladies and gentlemen. Kids. Kids. I hope you are enjoying your half-time event. We have another four-letter tradition here at the Fair Oaks High Prom. And that is a "song." Now it takes a special nine-letter word to make that song happen. And that word is "Don Hjelle." Don.

JOEL *brings a guitar for* DON's *abortive attempt of Bryan Adam's "(Everything I Do) I Do It for You".*

DON:
Look into my eyes
and you will see—Hold!
Look into my eyes
and you—Again.
Look into my eyes
and you will see—
Goddamnit. (CARSON *tries to reassure* DON.) Again.
Look into my eyes
and you will see
what you mean to me.
Search your heart.
Search your soul.
And when you find me there,
you'll search no more.

Don't tell me
it's not worth trying for.
You can't tell me
it's not worth dying for.
You know it's true.
Everything I do,
I do it for you.

STUDENTS *turn to face the audience.*

DON: *Look into your heart*
                        and you will find
                        there's nothing there to hide.
                        So, take me as I am.
                        Take my life.
                        I will give it all.
                        I would sacrifice.
                        Don't tell me
                        it's not worth fighting for.
                        I can't help it,
                        there's nothing I want more.
                        Yeah, I would fight for you.
                        I'd lie for you.
                        Walk the wire for you.
                        Yeah, I'd die for you!

STUDENTS *turn to face* DON.

DON: *You know it's true.*
                        Everything I do,
                        I do it for you.

SYLVIA *(taking the center of the playing field)*: All right, here we are.
    It's time for the coronation of the Fair Oaks High Prom King
    and Queen.

STUDENTS *go to their places for the march.*

SYLVIA *(to students)*: Five, six, seven, eight. March. *(To crowd.)* Coronation: A ceremony that hearkens back to those romantic Middle Ages when peasants were peasants and noblemen were "noble."

STUDENTS *are marching toward the mat.*

SYLVIA: And now I present to you, for your envy, your contempt, and for your evaluation, the 2006 Fair Oaks High School Prom Court!

MILO: Ooooh ... ooh ... oh ... ooh ...

PAULETTE *and* CARSON *dangle the crowns over the heads of the hopeful would-be kings and queens.* LEAH *and* RILEY *are crowned.*

The STUDENTS *part. The* REFEREE *uses a leaf blower to rid the mat of punch cups.*

The STUDENTS *enact a ritual coronation that culminates in a kiss that sends* RILEY *spinning into space. They part.*

UBER VOICE: At the Prom, there's an ever-present risk of delirium. At the Prom, it's either far too early or way too late. At the Prom, you're either on the dance floor or floating through space.

The CHAPERONES *huddle. The* REFEREE *signals for the game to continue.*

REFEREE *(grunting)*: Who's gonna make a play? It's time to correct the mistakes we've made in the past because the next twenty minutes are going to be the most important minutes of your life. Who's gonna be the one to say they were there when it all went down? Show some sack. It's gut check time. It's gut check time. Ladies and gentlemen, welcome to the second half. Rock and roll. *(Whistle.)*

CHAPERONES: Break!

UBER VOICE: Fast Dance Number Ten.
PAULETTE: *(Horn.)*

The STUDENTS *run to the dance floor.*

PAULETTE: *(Horn.)*

The STUDENTS *dance.*

PAULETTE: *(Horn.)*

Dancing ceases.

RILEY: GO!

The STUDENTS *huddle at the past end zone.*

NEIL: Five, six.
STUDENTS *(marching)*: Five, six, seven, eight. Let us go. Wish us well.
DON *(à la Braveheart)*: We cannot take their lives, but only we can give
    them their freedom!
STUDENTS: The future!

The STUDENTS *break for the FUTURE, not without resistance from the
chaperones. They succeed, say good-bye to the* Chaperones, *and proceed
to the door.*

RILEY: It's locked.
LEAH: It can't be locked.
RILEY: It's locked!
OTHERS: It can't be locked. *(And ad-libs.)*

The door is locked. The STUDENTS *are forced to come back into the room.*

REFEREE: *(Whistle.)* Goal: chaperones.

The STUDENTS *contest the call and* CHAPERONES *celebrate.*

MILO: Ladies and gentlemen, we are deep into the second half. It's
   getting late. Let's start looking ahead. I have always called talking
   about feelings "important talk." You hear the future beckoning
   you. *(Spotlights.)* The future is drowning, and it needs you to
   throw it a life preserver. I like to swim—but there are some days
   I just don't feel like doing it—but I do it anyway. Often when you
   think you are at the end of something, you are at the beginning
   of something else. *(Spotlights.)* Don't worry. Be prepared. And
   now to quote the dead Mr. Rogers:

MILO: Hey, are you ready?

CHAPERONES: Yeah, dawg, we're ready!

	Reach for the stars
	Shoot for the moon
	Do as I say, not as I do
	don't knock it till you try it
	if you break it then you buy it.
	Two wrongs don't make a right,
	but two Wrights made a plane
MILO:	Never say never
CHAPERONES:	whoop, there it is
	whoop, there it is
	always believe that you can achieve
	the goals and the dreams
	that your heart can conceive
	friends don't let friends
	Only you can prevent
	if at first you don't succeed
	this is your brain
	Learning happens.

RICH *throws the* STUDENTS *the keys. The* STUDENTS *don't know what to
do with them. The adults set up an additional row of seats.* RICH *gestures*

for them to sit in them. The CHAPERONES *and the* REFEREE *leave for the dressing rooms. The* STUDENTS *take their seats.*

UBER VOICE: The final slow dance. The night opens up.

VIKTOR *and* GRETCHEN *take the dance floor. Their lines are in voice-over.*

VIKTOR: *(Mario song.)* Say something to her. *(Makes video game noise.)* Come on, just one thing.

GRETCHEN: *(Video game noise.)* Who *is* this boy? He's such an odd little mouse.

VIKTOR: *(Video game noise.)* That chemistry teacher? Mr. Watchke? He's out to get me. Where is he?

GRETCHEN: And I'm a lonely egg, just a lonely egg . . .

VIKTOR: 'Cause, one time? That chemistry teacher humiliated me in class,

GRETCHEN: Put me down. I wish he'd put me down. I have a wedgie.

VIKTOR: Awww, it's these stupid pants. Crap, I should have worn cooler pants.

GRETCHEN: Uhh, this is impossible. My palms are all sweaty . . . I should stick to girls.

CHRISTIAN, TRACY, BROOKE, *and* NEIL *take the dance floor.*
In voice-over:

CHRISTIAN: Three years dating Brooke, and what do I have to show for it?

TRACY: Christian. There's nothing over there. Just boobs and two blank eyes. Stop looking!

BROOKE: I can't believe it. I'm going to study broadcast journalism at Northwestern. No more stupid Minnesota. I'm off to do the news at Northwestern!

CHRISTIAN: Man. I mean, what's with her? Why is she still a virgin when she's so totally hot? It's breaking my brain.

TRACY: Come on, Christian, don't be such a douche bag. I'll give you anything. Name it. You won the lottery.

BROOKE: Like, who did the sucky decorations in here? I'm all sweaty. I need to put on more perfume.

CHRISTIAN: High school's almost over, and I'm so tired of myself. Like, did I blow it? Will I ever get to be in love with anybody?

TRACY: Who's Brooke? She's like all beauty and perfect, perfect, perfect. Come on, you big lug. I'm the future.

BROOKE: I'm already five hundred miles away. Isn't life like so totally just the best?

NEIL: My father's a biologist—he came here from Ghana. My mother has MS—she's losing her eyesight. I didn't used to have much of a heart—I used to be a bully—but now I've lost weight, and I love my church. I *love* my church. These people don't know me. *(Short pause.)* I bet not a single person here knows anything about me.

JAZZLYN *and* RIKKI *take the dance floor. In voice-over:*

JAZZLYN: If my boyfriend were here, we'd show everybody. If my boyfriend were here, there'd be no room for doubt.

RIKKI: God, I miss Pete. He better not be out with that stupid chick from work. Why did I come to this? I hate these things.

JAZZLYN: If my boyfriend were here, I'd just lay it all down.

RIKKI: The music sucks. There's no booze . . . There's no place to talk.

JAZZLYN: If my boyfriend were here, we'd let everyone know that we are planning to live in Paris, and I'll dance with the ballet, and he'll start a business or something like that, and our children will speak French and nothing else but maybe Spanish at home.

RIKKI: I'll tell you one thing, I better not be pregnant.

JAZZLYN: 'Cause my boyfriend, he's got a very, *very* clear idea of the way things work. Period.

JOEL *and* LENI *take the dance floor. In voice-over:*

JOEL (*sings*): Daisy, Daisy, Give me your answer true.

LENI: I'm looking at two best friends. And they fall for each other in the cheesiest sort of way—at the prom. It's against all their principles.

JOEL (*sings*): I'm half crazy, all for the love of you.

LENI: So what are we looking at here? We're gonna distract each other for a few months?

JOEL (*sings*): It won't be a stylish marriage. I can't afford a carriage.

LENI: We're gonna end up in the lost love photo album.

JOEL: So Leni of the pizza with tuna fish and pickles, Leni of the farts in movie theaters, Leni of the desperate phone calls when romance crashes—I can't wait to see your eyes up real, real, real close.

LENI: It's not going to happen, is it? It shouldn't happen, should it? Should it?

LEAH *and* RILEY *take the dance floor. In voice-over:*

LEAH: I wonder if the reason

RILEY: That I feel so strange

LEAH: That I feel so strange is that

RILEY: I don't see an easy way out of here.

LEAH: I'm *hoping* for a better way out of here.

RILEY: The only *good* thing is

LEAH: Is I see him over there

RILEY: I see her over there and

LEAH: I know he'd give me more

RILEY: I know she'd give me more

LEAH: If we weren't so worried.

RILEY: Worried.

LEAH: About what's supposed to happen.

RILEY: Worried.

LEAH: About what's supposed to happen.

RILEY: If we weren't so worried about what's supposed to happen.

The STUDENTS *move to the dance floor and approach one another slowly, dancing. The* CHAPERONES *reenter, blindfolded, and lower the halo as the* STUDENTS *lie down on the mat.*

MILO (*singing*): Pretend you don't see them, my heart, although they are coming our way. Pretend you don't need them, my heart, but smile and pretend to be gay. It's too late for running, my heart. Chin up if the tears start to fall. Look somewhere above them, pretend you don't love them, pretend you don't see them at all.

REFEREE (*gestures a touchdown*): Goal: Students. Students survive the prom and create a past. The final score is declared irrelevant. The game is ended. The clock is still running.

The halo turns to become a passageway. MILO *begins to speak.*

MILO: Ladies and gentlemen, the last dance marks the end of the 2006 Fair Oaks High prom. We hope that you have been—well, you know. As the lights dim, and the last notes are played. Remember:

> change, if you consider it a constant, can be a comfort.
> change, if you consider it a constant, can be a comfort.
> change, if you consider it a constant, can be a comfort.
> change, if you consider it a constant, can be a comfort.
> change, if you consider it a constant, can be a comfort.

Good-byes. The STUDENTS *pass through the circle, greeting* MILO *as they pass.* MILO *gives* JOEL *the keys.*

UBER VOICE: The Prom is a mill that grinds the grain of the present into the flour of the future.

The STUDENTS *go to the FUTURE door. It is open. They pass through. The faculty exit upstage.*

MILO *approaches the center, rises out of his wheelchair, crosses through the ring, and reminisces about his prom.*

THE END.

ELISSA ADAMS is director of new play development at Children's Theatre Company. She has overseen the commissioning and development of more than twenty new plays at CTC since 1998, including *Esperanza Rising, Brooklyn Bridge, Once upon a Forest, A Very Old Man with Enormous Wings, Reeling, Five Fingers of Funk, Snapshot Silhouette, Korczak's Children,* and *Anon(ymous)*.

PETER BROSIUS has been artistic director of Children's Theatre Company since 1997. He directed the world premieres of *Bert and Ernie, Goodnight!, Iqbal, Madeline and the Gypsies, Average Family, The Lost Boys of Sudan, Anon(ymous), Reeling, The Monkey King, Hansel and Gretel, The Snow Queen,* and *Mississippi Panorama,* all commissioned and workshopped in CTC's new play development lab.

Award-winning playwright **LONNIE CARTER** is widely acclaimed for his hip-hop dialect and rhythms, syncopated poetry and prose, humor, pathos, and sharp social commentary. He has taught playwriting in the Dramatic Writing Program at New York University since 1979. More information about his work is available at www.lonniecarter.com.

NAOMI IIZUKA was born in Tokyo and raised in Japan, Indonesia, Holland, and Washington, D.C. She has received several prestigious playwriting awards, and her work has been produced and developed throughout the United States.

WHIT MᴀᴄLAUGHLIN is the OBIE and Barrymore Award–winning artistic director of New Paradise Laboratories. Since 1978, he has acted in, directed, or written more than one hundred theatre productions, most created in the midst of researching the techniques of collaborative theatre creation. To learn more about MacLaughlin and New Paradise Laboratories, go to www.newparadiselaboratories.org.

WILL POWER is an award-winning playwright and performer. Viewed as a pioneer in hip-hop theatre, he created his own style of theatrical communication, which fuses original music, rhymed language, and dynamic choreography. More information about him and his work can be found at http://willpower.tv.

CHILDREN'S THEATRE COMPANY (CTC), located in Minneapolis, Minnesota, is widely recognized as the leading theatre for young people and families in North America. Winner of the 2003 Tony® Award for regional theatre, CTC has received numerous honors, including awards from The Joyce Foundation and The Wallace Foundation. It participates in the National Endowment for the Arts New Play Development Program, the Shakespeare for a New Generation program, the EmcArts Innovation Lab funded by the Doris Duke Charitable Foundation, and the New Voices/New Visions 2010 series presented by The John F. Kennedy Center for the Performing Arts. CTC serves more than 250,000 people annually through performances, new play development, theatre arts training, and community and education programs. For more information about Children's Theatre Company, visit www.childrenstheatre.org.